PATTERSON HEIGHTS

Felicia Pride

PATTERSON HEIGHTS

Recycling programs
for this product may
not exist in your area.

PATTERSON HEIGHTS

ISBN-13: 978-0-373-83148-7

www.KimaniTRU.com

Printed in U.S.A.

Thank you: God. My mother. My family and loved ones. My agent, Adrienne Ingrum. My editor, Evette Porter, and the Kimani TRU team. My friends. My colleagues. Baltimore.

prologue

timed out

TIME is funny. Not ha-ha funny like those silly co-medians who come on late-night cable. Time is funny, like funny-acting. It'll switch up on you like a friend who steals your girl. One minute you're a little kid copping candy at the corner store with your big brother and the next minute you're at his funeral wondering if tears run out.

That's why I've lost respect for time. I used to count the number of minutes that my peoples spent arguing in the next room—how often Moms yelled at Pops for the wildest reasons—because he failed to call her when he was supposed to, or he left his socks in the middle of the living room floor, or because he wouldn't get out of the car to pay respects to his dead son.

But I've lost count. Or lost the desire to count. Not sure which one. It didn't take me long to realize that the time my parents wasted being mad at each other didn't mean spit. Five minutes versus fifteen, no difference. A fight is a fight regardless of how long it lasts. Death is permanent no matter if it happened yesterday or if it took place a year ago. That realization came to me the hard way.

Time is funny. It'll flip on you.

One minute you're part of the perfect family, or at least, the family that's perfect for you. Mine didn't have tons of money, didn't live in one of those big houses in the County, but we had each other, and that was enough for me. But in a matter of seconds, that unit was smashed into unidentifiable pieces. My family, as I once knew it, no longer exists. That's time for you.

You could say that time and I are beefing. Hard. If I could, I'd grab seconds, minutes and hours by the neck and force them to follow my lead. Do what I told them to do. I'd blast time in its back and force it to erase itself. I am tired of time kicking my butt up and down life.

In between blocking out the yells of my parents and thinking about the downward spiral of my life—the death of the family I once knew, the constant threats to my budding manhood and the girl who's got my mind doing backflips—I've come up with a master plan. I am going to steal time away from time.

I am going to start over.

Forget the fact that I have spent the last fifteen years in a life that I can no longer recognize. If the people on those talk shows with messed-up lives can put the past behind them and start new, I figure so can I. Same name. Same parents. Different Avery Washington. I might not be able to completely erase time, but I can put a serious dent into its plans.

It's like a rebirth. But honestly, I don't care what you call it. All that matters is that things are going to be different. Life, my life will be different.

The new Avery isn't going to be bound by anyone's rules, not even my parents'. They have reached a new level in blocking a brother's freedom. My mother thinks lockdown is the best way to protect her only remaining son—so scared that I might end up dead that she doesn't want me walking to the mailbox without knowing my every move. Forget the fact that I am almost grown. And Pops is too tired to stick up for me. I am on my own.

So check it. The new Avery is going to pass out ass whippings like party fliers. Let that gangsta wannabe Billy try to punk me again like he did the first week of school, or let that clown Dante think about getting buck. I had beat downs with their names on them. Oh and let Natasha try to get in my face like she really gives a rat's ass about me. I'm gonna let her have it, too.

The new me also has the balls to roll up on my brother's murderer the next time our paths cross. I used to think that Rashid wouldn't want me to score revenge, but hell, I also used to believe in justice and my mother's plea to let the police and the courts handle everything. After months without progress, I've realized that I have been looking at everything all wrong. It's time for me to man up and protect all that is left: my brother's legacy. Every time Rashid's murderer walks the streets he is stomping on my brother's life. The new Avery is prepared to handle business.

Think of it as kind of like the ugly, slow caterpillar becoming the cool and free butterfly. It's like a video in science class. It looks kind of nasty. Maybe a better example is the nerdy and weak Clark Kent hitting up the phone booth and becoming Superman, the savior.

Here's the truth: If Rashid was still breathing, things would be very different. Life would have continued as usual. But I couldn't go back in time. I could only go forward.

It is time. Time to regain time lost and time wasted. I ain't afraid to shred my former self. I don't have lint to lose. All the rage, anger and pressure that I have been holding on to like an emotional storage unit—

trying to be the good son, good student and good guy all at the same time, in a bad world—is going to be thrown out the window like days-old trash.

Today is the first day of my life.

one

THE LONGEST DAY of their LIVES

It was Sunday, the Lord's day; an unusually cool morning in July that gave all of Baltimore a break from the clothes-sticking heat. No ghetto birds or sirens. No pop-pops or beef-defining ruckus. The city echoed. Baltimore was resting.

The sun shined brightly into my room. Rashid and I had stayed up late battling on Xbox and eating crab chips. My head pounded, punishing me for getting only three hours of sleep. But skipping service was not going to happen in the Washington household. My parents were adamant that every Sunday, the entire clan—all four of us—were present at New

Saints Tabernacle's 9:00 am service. Church was my parents' way of keeping our lives in order.

I could hear the shower through the thin rowhouse walls. The bathroom was sandwiched between me and my brother's rooms. I was thankful that big bro was giving me a few more minutes to chill in the bed, although that wasn't easy to do with Mom's strawberry pancakes calling my name like one of the cuties at me and Rashid's school.

A bang at the door knocked my senses.

"Your turn," Rashid yelled through the door before heading to his room to finish getting ready. He didn't have one of those deep voices but the fellas around the way still listened when Rashid talked. Some of his boys joked and called him young Barack because he could make even the most ignorant cat pause and think. I didn't tell anyone this, but sometimes I would practice making my voice sound like his. It didn't work.

It took me another few minutes to convince my body to get up. I slowly rolled out of bed like a car on the creep and went to check my brother before getting clean.

He was shining his shoes like somebody's grandfather, a task I hated but one he did every week. Our father had taught us, told my brother and I that clean shoes were a sign of a man in control. I didn't really think that was true, but I guessed my brother did.

"Yo, we should wear the new shirts we copped from Macy's," I suggested. Rashid nodded his head in agreement.

"Oh most definitely," he said as he brushed his shoes. "You know how we do. I already ironed them, playboy." He pointed over to the pale blue and light green shirts that were hung neatly in front of Rashid's closet door. Not one wrinkle in sight. We used part of the money we made at Moe's Car Wash to buy the shirts. They were on sale for twenty-five dollars each. Rashid said we were getting a crazy deal because they were made by some designer dude with a name I couldn't pronounce.

"The honeys gonna be on us," I said confidently, although I was really only hopeful.

"You better hop in the shower before Moms come in here getting on you."

"You right." I grabbed my shirt and headed to the bathroom.

It wasn't long before Rashid and I were fighting over our mother's smoked bacon while Pops was reading aloud all the depressing articles from the *Baltimore Sun*.

"Man shot dead. Economy in the toilet. Test scores at an all-time low. This is the world we live in," he announced. He was rocking his reading glasses at the bottom of his nose like a teacher. Pops had dropped out of high school, but eventually got his GED. He was the smartest guy I knew, even smarter than my teachers. He was always reading books or newspapers and telling Rashid and I about things going on in the world. "Learning is a lifelong process," he would say to us.

But I was tired of always hearing about the bad stuff going on in Baltimore. Rashid and I had become used to the messed-up headlines. After a while, all the murders, wars and disease became just that, words on paper.

"Look at my sons looking good," Moms bragged. She bent down and hugged her boys simultaneously. Strands of the brown hair that she dyed red fell gently onto our heads. Like every Sunday, she was dressed in office attire—blouse and skirt—that she wore to her desk job at Social Security.

"Well you know how we do," Rashid said as he brushed his shoulder. I followed. With our new shirts, we had on some crisp black slacks and matching dress shoes. So fresh, so clean.

"We make some handsome kids." My father patted Moms on the butt. "When are we going to get working on a little girl?" he said jokingly. They kissed like it was the first time their lips ever touched. Some kids thought it was nasty to see their parents kissing or talking about getting it on, but I didn't mind. I would much rather have them all in each other's face than to be arguing like they hate each other. Too many of my friends lived in single-parent homes. I knew Rashid and I were lucky.

"Dad got game," Rashid joked as he gave Pops a pound. I laughed at the thought of our father being a ladies' man. It was clear that I got my looks from him. He was a few inches shorter than Moms. He and I shared a wide nose, eyes made for old men and a bubble forehead. Rashid on the other hand favored our mom—her tightly curled hair, welcoming eyes and small set of freckles. Chicks always asked Rashid about the brown dots on his face. The ladies thought they were cute.

"Now you know, if we have a little girl, she going to have you wrapped around her little finger," Moms said as she hugged Pops tightly.

"Man, I don't know if I can deal with having a younger sister," Rashid jumped in. "That means I'm gonna have to keep all the cats around the way out of her face. None of them would have the chance to try to disrespect her." Rashid pounded his fist into his hand for emphasis. I nodded my head in agreement. Rashid wasn't a fighter, one of those guys who would rumble for the stupidest stuff, but he stood up for what was right.

"You know it," I said while drowning my bacon in syrup.

There were a few times when Rashid came to my rescue in elementary school when older boys were trying to clown me. Being small made me an easy target.

"Y'all know this my brother, right?" he'd say. Kids would nod their heads. "You got a problem with him? You got a problem with me." Cats would usually mumble something like, "You know we cool, Rashid. We was just messing with Lil' Avery." They'd give me a fake pound and move on. I didn't care if they meant it. I felt good that my big bro put them in their place.

"Both of you would make perfect big brothers." My mother kissed our foreheads. Rashid's first, then mine. She once told us that every time she looked at us, she saw perfection, even when we weren't acting perfect.

The four of us sat around the kitchen table and continued to joke around. It was an easy Sunday morning.

Everything about New Saints was small—the size of its old brick building, the amount of members in its congregation and our short pastor who was often mistaken for one of the teenagers when his back was turned. But my family liked that. The church was always at the center of important events in our lives. My mother loved to retell the story of how, on a rainy day in September, it was at New Saints that nineteen-year-old Yvette Anderson and twenty-one-year-old

James Washington, high school sweethearts, got married. Two years later, the young couple baptized their first son there, whom they named Rashid after a mutual friend who hooked them up. Another two years later, they baptized me, their second son, whose name they took from a character in one of my mother's favorite books, *The Color Purple*.

My brother and I grew up in New Saints. Everyone knew us: the two well-behaved big-headed Washington boys. Going to church wasn't really a chore to us, mainly because New Saints had the prettiest girls. The girls never disappointed by wearing their cute dresses that showed a nice amount of leg.

And because of Rashid's lively and passionate drum playing—he was known to completely zone out, eyes shut, head bobbing hard to his own beat—my brother was a minicelebrity. Although he was supposed to be playing for the glory of the Lord, the fast girls in the congregation all thought he was rocking praise and worship for them. That made me famous by association.

That morning, we sat in our usual pew, fourth row on the left. Every week, the program was the same. Service started with greetings and fellowship. That's when we got to go around and hug everyone. And of course, Rashid and I made sure we hit up the cuties.

"So nice to see you this weekend, Sister Regina,"

Rashid said to one of the finest girls in church. Rashid called her a twenty because she was two *dimes* in one.

"Nice to see you, too, Brother Rashid. Did you have a good week?"

"Always," he said as he held her hand longer than necessary. He flashed her one of his golden smiles and she blushed like she was in elementary school. I stood next to him taking mental notes. I was trying to get my game on Rashid's level.

After chatting with everyone, it was time for praise and worship. It was Rashid's Sunday to bless the drums and that morning, he was on fire, banging the instruments with passion and purpose like he was trying to speak through his music. The beat pounded through the small church like a car's bass. Everyone felt it. His solo made Sister Thomasina jump out of her seat and perform her holy two-step. Pops was nodding his head, man-style. My mother yelled, "That's my son," like she was at one of his basketball games and everyone didn't already know that.

"Thank the Lord for our band!" Reverend Sullivan said when they finished. "Our young Brother Rashid has a God-given talent to make the drums come alive, doesn't he?" The congregation gave a collective amen.

When Rashid returned, my mother gave him a big kiss on his cheek and Pops gave him a hug. I gave him a pound.

"Did I do okay?" he asked me.

"Man, you tore it up!" I told him. He smiled. Even with all the applause he received, my opinion mattered to him.

After New Saints had calmed down from the lively praise and worship, there was offering. Rashid and I agreed to put in ten dollars a week between the two of us. It was his idea. "Yo, we'll get back ten times the amount we put in," he said to convince me when we first started last year.

Then came announcements, the sermon, more prayer and depending on how long that last prayer session lasted—which usually depended on how many people were sick, needed to repent for the sins of the week or wanted to give their life to God— church lasted about two hours. Then there was the after-service lingering when the whole family made the rounds to chat with everyone we hadn't seen in a week. Rashid was showered with compliments about his drum playing and everybody congratulated me for being accepted into the accelerated academic program at Baltimore Central High. Rashid and I left church feeling ourselves.

Soon as we got home, Rashid changed out of his sharp church clothes and threw on blue balling shorts, an old pair of Air Jordans and a white tank top. He was built like a college freshman guard. Not too tall, with small muscular arms and bony legs. The heat didn't stop him from hitting the courts on Sundays.

My basketball skills were sloppy at best, though Rashid was never embarrassed by them. He would always pick me first on his team.

"Damn, why you choose him?" cats would say to Rashid. "I mean, he's your brother, but he's sorry."

"You said it, he's my brother. You got a problem with him being on the team, switch sides," he'd reply.

So I usually did homework, played Xbox to get my skills up or took a nap while Rashid was hooping. That day, I decided on the latter. Sleep was the most perfect state of being. No thinking. No doing. No feeling. Sleep and I got along real well. Rashid thought I spent too much time in the bed versus experiencing life. "I'll have time to sleep when I'm dead," he would always tell me.

"Sure you don't want to come and get your ball on?" he asked me before jetting out the house. I was sure. We made plans to battle on Xbox after Rashid did his thing.

Before leaving, he gave Pops a pound and kissed Moms on the forehead. Our parents were watching an infomercial for some expensive-ass vacuum cleaner.

After changing into gym shorts from the previous school year, I hopped in the bed and dreamt about Beyoncé dropping it.

two

Lowdown

They say a fight broke out between hot-headed Darryl and Trevor, Peety's son. They say Darryl started it. Kept callin' Trevor out for missing shots and rebounds. They say Trevor kept cool, but Darryl kept talking trash. They say Rashid came between Darryl and Trevor a few times during the game and kept the peace. Cats went back to playing. They say that when the game was over, all 250 pounds of Darryl pushed Trevor's 165 pounds to the ground. They say Darryl told Trevor that he'd better not come back to the courts with that sorry game. They say Trevor remained silent. Bounced. Cats left the court. Started walking home. They say Trevor returned with his dignity and a .22. They say he shot like a rookie at the group of boys heading to the corner store. Aimed for Darryl. Hit Rashid. They say the few kids who hung around after the game were ghost after the shots were fired. They say Rashid hit the sidewalk with a loud thump. Trevor didn't watch to see his victim fall. When the men in blue arrived minutes later, the streets were vacant. When 5-0 went around knocking on doors for answers, *they* didn't say anything.

three

man up

shooting that kid was the first time I had fired a gun, although I had imagined the day several times in my mind. After that last assault from Darryl, I heard my father's angry voice in my head. "Man up, Trevor," he yelled.

So I did. At least I thought that was what I was doing. I hurried down the block like I was trying to catch up to something. I reached my 2005 black Lexus ES, a gift courtesy of my father's thriving business. My hands were shaking, so it took me longer than usual to open the passenger side. I reached under the seat and felt for the .22 my father had given me as a belated birthday present.

I didn't like playing with toy guns as a child. I preferred crayons, newspaper and imagination. I could paint my butt off. Thugs around the way may have looked down on it, but they ain't say anything. I was still Peety's son. The girls loved me for it. Not only was I a baller without having to be a baller, but I could also whip up a portrait of a shorty and give it as a gift. By the next day me and the breezy of the week were getting familiar.

Peety tried several times to recruit me into the family business. The same business his incarcerated father, O. G. Mick Rock, passed down to him before his life sentence in prison. But I was a seventeen-year-old who preferred being at school to sitting around with a bunch of mofos doing nothing at one of my father's stash houses. At least in school there were some cute chicks going places. I liked hollering at the college-bound even if higher education wasn't a part of the plan. My father wouldn't pay for school unless I joined the organization (that's what my father called it) and went to school solely to learn more about the business. I wanted to study art. My father laughed at my punk-ass ambitions and told me I better smarten up. It was that same voice that I heard the last time Darryl stripped me of my dignity.

I pointed the gun in Darryl's direction, but closed my eyes when I pulled the trigger. I didn't want to see the bullet hit its target. My hands were trembling like an addict needing a fix. But I did it. I blasted. The kickback caught me off guard. I didn't realize it was going to be so strong.

Part of me wanted my father to be there to prove that I had what it took, but I was more relieved that he wasn't there to see my sloppy performance. Deep down inside I just wanted to scare Darryl for trying to punk me. But I hit one. Not even the right one— the one who was trying to cool everyone down. The moment I saw him catch the bullet, I ran. The gun felt like hellfire in my hand, but I knew that I couldn't drop it. My father would have to dispose of it. I stashed it in my shorts and hopped in my car.

After changing the course of several lives, the first thing I did was pray, although you'd never catch me in a church unless it was for a funeral. I only remembered praying the day my mother was shot and killed in front of me. But I was a few seconds from taking my own life with the same gun. I asked for forgiveness even though I didn't think I deserved it. Thirty seconds later, I pulled off and drove away from death.

I flipped open my phone and dialed my father's number. I wondered if anything would come out if I tried to speak.

"What up?" Peety answered with real irritation in his voice.

"I have to see you." I was surprised how the words flowed and how I remembered not to give out any incriminating details over the phone.

"You know where to meet me," Peety barked before hanging up. He hated phones.

I headed to one of my father's downtown row houses. Weaving the Lex in and out of traffic, passing the Sunday drivers and going around the cars double-parked outside of churches, I arrived twelve minutes later at the spot. I was breathless and fearful.

The place looked rough and shabby on the outside, but was totally different on the inside. The rowhouse looked like it should have been demolished with the other half-dozen bordered-up houses that sat hopelessly on the block. When you got past the broken screen door, the seemingly vacant house was decked out with flat-screen televisions, a room-sized pool table and leather couches. Well, just on the first floor. The rest of the house was empty, except for the king-sized bed in one corner of the second-floor bedrooms, which was for Peety's extracurricular activities. No one lived there. It was just a place to hang, drink, smoke.

Peety pulled up in a black Suburban. Alone. I was relieved. Peety was always crazier around his peoples. He parked and motioned for me to get out of the car. We walked around the back of the house into the alley.

"Where's the gun?" Peety asked with a twisted fatherly intuition. But Peety was psychic like that. He knew when a rival hustler was setting him up. He knew when my mother was pregnant before she did. He knew when his brother was going to walk away from the game. And for that reason, he thought he was untouchable. "I'm gonna see them coming before they get a chance to come at me," he'd tell his people.

I handed him the brown paper bag that I had stashed the weapon in.

After confirming that I had given him the right weapon, Peety gave me dap followed by a shoulder hug.

I tried hard to avoid what was about to happen, but my soul won out. Tears started rolling down my baby face.

"Why you crying?" Peety barked. With his white wifebeater and matching sweats, Peety looked like your average B'more cat. He preferred to blend in rather than stand out. Only a few people really knew what he looked like and he worked to keep it that way. He took a swig from his water bottle. Water kept him sharp.

"They all saw me," I cried uncontrollably. "I think he's dead," I said apologetically.

"He deserved to be handled," Peety said. "I'm proud of you. You protected the family name. You stood your ground and didn't let some fool punk you."

"I didn't hit the right person," I managed to get out.

"What you mean you didn't hit the right person?" Peety looked at me, confused.

"I shot the wrong person," I repeated, this time in a voice so high that it cracked.

Peety grabbed his firstborn by the neck. "Stop being a lil' bitch. Tell me what happened. Don't leave nothing out."

I told him what happened. My father was pissed, but then he told me that it was part of the game. "Shit happens," was the way he responded. Then he told me to chill out. He'd handle business.

A few days later, Peety handled business. He arranged for me to take a short vacation.

"Ain't no thang, you'll be back and everything will be back to normal," Peety said to me, as I slid into D-Block's Range Rover. Peety closed the passenger door.

"You ready, playa?" my father's henchman asked. I nodded. I thought about sleeping for the entire ride, but sleep meant seeing the kid's face. So I focused on the road, the white lines, the yellow ones, and wondered if his image would ever fade away.

I had spent my short time on Earth trying to earn my father's respect. Once I got it, I no longer wanted it. But I knew I still had to play the part around my father. Inside I was damaged. I no longer dreamed. All my mind could muster were nightmares. Rising in the morning and facing another day made me sick. I'd see his face and start shaking. But that didn't matter. In three months' time, I'd return to East Baltimore.

four

clairvoyant

---

teeny's mother, Ms. Rosalie, was the one who delivered the news. By the time she did, Rashid had already died in the ambulance on the way to the hospital.

She was folding clothes at the time. Her hair was still in rollers and would remain that way throughout the day. Sunday was time to attack household chores. Although her sons were all old enough to match up their socks and wash their own underwear, she still enjoyed taking care of her boys.

When her youngest ran into the house, a firestorm of fury and sadness, Ms. Rosalie knew death had just hit East Baltimore. Again. She could see the future that way, a gift she gained from her years working as a high school teacher over West.

"Catch your breath, son, and tell me what happened," she said as calmly as she could.

"Rashid, Rashid," was all that came out. She hadn't seen her son cry like a toddler since he was a toddler. The tears were uncontrollable. Her heart was breaking.

She grabbed the back of the sofa for balance. Her legs were weakening, giving out. She had known Rashid before he could speak. She and Yvette had become friends raising good black boys in a harsh world. Rashid had given Michael his nickname, Teeny, when they were youngsters on the school playground—a harmless tag that reflected the fact that Teeny was nearly triple the weight of his classmates.

Tears invaded Ms. Rosalie's eyes. She let them fall.

"Rashid, what happened to Rashid?" she asked although she already knew the answer. Teeny couldn't respond although he wanted to. His heart was pounding too loudly.

She gathered the energy to grab the cordless phone from the coffee table and dial 911. She reported a shooting, following her son's head nods as cues. The police were already made aware and were on their way. She dropped the phone. It was heavy in her hand.

Her son was still hysterical.

"Trevor, Trevor," he said between pants and cries.

She grabbed her son tightly to her chest like she used to do when he was a child and was upset. He laid his head on her shoulder and their hearts began to beat together. She needed to slow him down. Calm him down. Let him know he was loved and he was safe. She gently stroked his cornrows. She let him be vulnerable. They rocked back and forth.

Ms. Rosalie didn't agree with how the streets operated, but she abided by their rules anyway. She knew Trevor was Peter's son, as she called him. She came up with Peter's father back in the day when gangsters were still gangsters, just a different breed.

As mother and son rocked, she opened her eyes and zeroed in on a family picture that sat on the windowsill. It was taken at Sears some years back when her three boys were just babies. They were still her babies. She whispered in the ear of her youngest not to say anything to anyone, including the police and especially to Avery and his family. After a few minutes, she picked up the phone once again and made the call she never thought she'd have to make.

five

broken

MY mother had just finished drying the dishes that my father had washed. She had put her foot into Sunday dinners—complete with cheesy macaroni and cheese (the way Rashid liked it), tender roast beef (the way Pops preferred), spicy collard greens (my favorite) and banging cornbread—the kind that melts in your mouth. We were waiting for Rashid to come home so we could eat together—another family thing we did every Sunday.

She answered the phone with a giggle because she had just popped Dad with the dish towel.

"Get a room," I told them.

"Hey, Rosalie," my mother said with the phone to her ear and a glass in her hand.

I guess Ms. Rosalie hadn't said anything, so my mother said "Hello" again before getting a response.

"Is everything okay?" my mother asked as she smacked my father's hand from her banana pudding. "You sound concerned."

Rosalie wasn't usually the quiet type. She always had something to say about something, especially when that something wasn't important. Now it was important and she could barely get out the words.

"You having problems with your phone," my mom said. "I'm going to hang up and I'll try to call you right back."

"No, I'm here," Rosalie finally uttered. "I don't know how to say this."

"You're scaring me, Rosalie." My father looked at Moms. He moved closer to her and rubbed her arm. I turned around and felt the mood shift too.

"Something has happened to Rashid," Rosalie blurted out as she started bawling. "He was just shot." The last words somersaulted out of Rosalie's mouth and hit like a punch to the stomach.

The glass Moms was drying shattered to the floor along with the telephone and her heart. An emotional hurricane hit her and she couldn't breathe. My father caught her from behind as she stumbled toward the floor.

"Honey, what's wrong?" Dad's eyes looked like

tunnels. I tried to travel through them. I was lost. I decided to help him calm my mother.

"Rashid," she sang in a weird melodious voice. "Rashid," was all she kept saying. Once we got her into a chair at the kitchen table, my father leaped to the phone to find out what made my mom's face turn a bluish color. Ms. Rosalie was on the other end crying loud enough that I could hear her. He slammed the phone onto the cradle, gathered us and we all jumped in the car.

"It's your brother, son. He's been shot." My father took a moment to tell me why we were leaving our perfectly good meal on the dining room table to rush to the hospital. The words didn't quite reach me. Instead, they just hung there. In the air. They reached my mother again. She screamed loudly. I still didn't get it.

Not one of us could remember the ten-minute ride to the hospital. Nor could we remember what we said when we arrived.

It didn't matter. Rashid had been pronounced dead before we got there. We missed his smile by twenty-two minutes.

My mother would have been hysterical, yelling at doctors, demanding that the nurses get answers, but she didn't have the energy. Her entire body was numb. She looked like one of the mannequins in a store window.

My father handled all the paperwork, questions and decisions. He went through the motions as if it was business as usual. But I knew he was just trying to be strong for us.

My young mind couldn't wrap around the fact that my brother, whom I had just seen hours earlier, who had just did his thing on the drums at church, was no longer. Disbelief felt comforting to me for the time being. It blocked reality.

We camped out at the hospital that night. My back began to hurt from sitting in the hard chairs in the waiting area. There were a few other people there, too. A white family was waiting on an older man who had a heart attack. The daughter looked around my age. Her eyes were all red and puffy from crying. I began to wonder where my tears were. Even when I was in the room with Rashid, it felt like he was asleep and I was waiting for him to wake up.

But all I could think about was Rashid. No real memories, just the image of him in his basketball shorts, the way I last saw him.

My father eventually cried a little. I counted three tears that rolled down his face when we sat in the hospital room staring at Rashid. Two from his left eye, one from the right. My mother held her dead son until the nurses would no longer let her.

That day, she lost her faith in God. Every Sunday from then on, she worshipped at Rashid's grave.

SIX

really real

I thought I had dreamed it. The cold hospital. My brother in the bed, dead. My mother's ghostly behavior. My father's quiet pain. But it couldn't have been a dream because you can't dream if you haven't slept.

After crashing at the hospital until my parents and I were forced to leave, I went straight for Rashid's room like I always did.

I wondered where my brother was. Maybe that's when reality set in, but I don't think so. I realized that Rashid was gone, but I didn't realize that he was *gone*.

The room was empty, but not lifeless. The bright yellow walls that Rashid and I painted one weekend to celebrate his favorite basketball team, the Lakers, made the room unusually sunny in a dark time. Rashid's Nike Airs that he had just cleaned the morning before with an old toothbrush sat in the corner on a copy of the *City Paper*.

I looked around like I was in a museum—admiring my brother's possessions—viewing them as if I had never seen them before, as if they were priceless.

While crossing the room, my foot got caught in the pile of clothes living on the floor. I picked up one of my brother's jerseys and smelled it. A mix of Rashid's knockoff Sean John cologne and the odor from spending too much time chilling outside in the heat made me remember him for a few seconds.

I took a moment and sat on his bed. Being in his room was both comforting and exhausting. I felt deathly tired. I swung my feet onto the bed so I could lie down and take in what was left of my brother in the room's air. I inhaled like a doctor was asking me to—big and dramatic.

I was trying to reminisce, but still no memories surfaced. My mind was blank and heavy. The vibration from my cell phone kept disturbing my state of nothingness. Under different circumstances I would have been pumped over the amount of texts and phone calls coming through. But the messages were mostly from Rashid's friends offering electronic condolences and asking about the funeral. I thought for a minute about throwing the flip phone up against the wall. At least if it was destroyed, I wouldn't have to deal with all the emotion. But I remembered that the phone was purchased using me and Rashid's shared savings—a crumbled collection of ones, fives, tens and twenties—that we received as tips from the ballers down at the car wash. Rashid wouldn't want me wasting our hard-earned money. I hit the Off button instead and closed my eyes.

seven

the choice is yours

our house had never been so packed with friends, family and neighbors—not during the celebrations following me and Rashid's accomplishments. Not on the day that Rashid's middle school basketball team won a championship or for the cookout congratulating me for being Student of the Year. Pops had to bring extra brown metal chairs up from the basement. I looked around at both the recognizable and strange faces and thought it was amazing or messed up, how death, not life, brought people together.

A low murmur of crying filled the small house. The familiar smell of home-cooked soul food donated by neighbors provided a little comfort. But my house still felt like an indoor cemetery.

Tavon grabbed my arm and led me to my bedroom. He was our big cousin—the one who let me and Rashid sip on our first beer and showed us our first set of titties in a porno magazine. Even though we thought Tavon knew better than to make prison his occasional home, we still thought he was one of the smartest and funniest dudes we knew. He was always spitting out random facts that he'd pick up watching stuff on the History or Discovery channel. He collected info on all types of things from how lions do it to why it is hot in the winter. "It's called global warming," he'd say. "Our planet is mad messed up, yo."

But on that night, he was his gutter self—wicked eyes matched the thirst of a hungry vampire. His white tee was muddy like he had been playing touch football at the park. He wasn't even rocking any of his diamonds—studs or medallions. I thought I saw a bulge under his shirt and became scared of what was coming next. Tavon had been riding around the hood getting answers.

"Say the word and it's done," Tavon whispered to me as we stood only breaths away from one another.

"What?" I asked in an attempt to stall for time. I sat down slowly on my bed and smoothed the brown sheets. I was trying to think, but my mind stopped working. What would Rashid do?

Tavon gave me a dumb look. He knew that I understood what he was talking about.

"You the man on this one," Tavon told me. "This is you. Rashid was my cousin, but he was yo brotha. You make the final call. This time around you the lieutenant and I'm the soldier. What's your order?"

My mind was spinning like the rims Rashid and I cleaned at the car wash. Visions of my brother flooded my brain. The two of us sitting on the stoop watching the honeys go past. The two of us at school cracking jokes in the cafeteria. I thought my brain was going to fall out of my head and my heart felt like it had stopped working.

"How did it happen? Who did it?" I asked.

"Word is the fool Darryl pissed Trevor off. You know, Peety's son." I nodded. "So Trevor leaves the court, comes back with the gat and starts blasting. Rashid got hit by accident."

The word "hit" didn't seem strong enough to describe what really happened to my brother. Tavon's words seemed to have rocked the house. I felt the ground move under me. Going after Peety's son would be a suicide mission for Tavon. Peety was notoriously big in the drug game. Knee-deep. But he was known more for bodies than he was for the ridiculous amounts of heroin he pumped through Baltimore. Rumors floated through the streets: Peety shot his best friend when he was twelve for stealing twenty dollars.

Peety's crew slaughtered a family of four—mother, father and two toddlers—because the mother spoke out against the drug activity on her street. Peety shot himself to prove to the world that he could take a bullet.

No one really knew what was true and what wasn't. But all of East Baltimore knew two things for sure: 1) Peety was crazier than his crazy father who ran B'more's streets before and after crack. 2) Don't mess with anything that got Peety's name on it—which included his broads, his kids, his money, his cars, his properties, his blocks, his businesses. None of it.

I couldn't answer, so I just waved my hands in a motion that said I surrendered.

"No?" Tavon asked me for confirmation.

I shook my head.

"You know who killed your brother and you ain't doin' nothing about it?" Tavon asked me with spitfire.

"I can't take more death." I paused, unsure if I should continue. "We'll go to the police," I added.

"A, that's not how the hood works. You know what happens to snitches?" It was a question that I wasn't supposed to answer and one that I didn't want to think about too hard. "The police can't do nothing about nothing. The moment Peety finds out that your family went to the police, you're all done. Darryl's ass bounced. Peety already put word on the street that nobody knows nothing. Plus Peety got them expensive-ass lawyers."

In a twisted way, Tavon was making sense.

"Loo, we'll let shit die down a little and then hit up that fool and make it look like he was jacked."

Tavon could see the concern on my face. He should have known that I didn't have the heart to order an execution. He dropped his head for a moment.

"Aiight, yo. Look, don't say nothing," Tavon warned me. His eyes burned through me.

Then my cousin turned around and left me with a heavy mind.

That night, I replayed the scene in my head and questioned my decision. Was I a punk for not retaliating? Did it matter that Trevor was Peety's son? Was it wrong that the thought of killing Rashid's murderer didn't make me feel any better? Was it okay that I wanted justice, just not in that way?

I was almost certain that Rashid wouldn't want me to sacrifice our cousin in the name of revenge. Rashid wouldn't have wanted his younger brother caught up in a beef that I would never be equipped to handle. Going up against Peety was like East Baltimore battling the entire country.

But I thought about seeing Trevor again. I've seen him only a few times around town and never thought much about it. Me and Rashid thought Trevor was cool, and fell far from the Peety tree. That thought messed with me. I remembered the last time I saw Trevor—at work, alongside my brother.

"Man, we both going to college," Rashid said as he shined the tires on a rimmed-up Range. We were drying the cars that rolled through Moe's Car Wash. Summer Saturdays at the spot were like outdoor block parties. Ballers, hustlers and half-naked chicks hung outside like it was a club at midnight. The sun beat down on us like an angry father. Our blue Moe's shirts were drenched with sweat.

"I just need to get my grades up," Rashid said. "But I ain't worried, 'cause you a genius and some of your smarts are going to rub off on me. You're going to be my tutor."

"Cool," I said with a cheesy grin. I wiped my wet hands on his T-shirt.

"We're going to get scholarships and everything," Rashid said as he continued the fantasy. "I'm telling you," he added as he touched my shoulder to let me know that he wasn't playing.

"Yo, check out the Cayenne." Thomas gleamed when the Porsche SUV pulled up for the super max wash. He also worked up Moe's and jocked anything he didn't own, which was about everything. Rashid wasn't impressed. With all the hot rides that rolled through on any given Saturday, he was never drooling over any of them.

"Yeah, the ride is tight, but what homie had to do to get it?" he'd say to the fellas whenever their eyes popped with desire.

"What up, playboy. You got my wheels good?" J-Block said as Rashid finished his tires. Everyone knew he worked for Peety doing whatever needed to be done. Lil' Man should have been his name, 'cause he only stood like five feet tall. Being little didn't matter, though, because everyone knew he toted big guns. J-Block acted like an immortal comic book character, impervious to bullets or life sentences. Most fools like him were eventually killed or staring at the walls of a tight, gray cell. J-Block gave life the middle finger.

"You know it, main man." Rashid gave him a pound. Rashid didn't care for J-Block, but he was cool with everyone. He knew that J-Block had a short temper and would take the smallest slights as a sign of disrespect. Rashid knew the value of life. He'd let the little things slide when the code of the streets demanded that young black men take everything to heart. To the minor shoulder bump, Rashid would reply, "Yo, you cool, don't worry about it." To the shit-talker who tried to test Rashid's patience, "You ain't worth it." He knew the real stakes at play that went beyond a reputation. He knew that life could change in mere seconds. Rashid respected time.

"Got the rims sparkling so you can be stuntin'

even harder." Rashid wiped down the tires of J-Block's brand-new black Range Rover one last time. In the sun, the SUV shone like a big-ass stallion. It was a sweet ride. So sweet that chicks were salivating over it like it was a piece of chocolate cake. They wanted a bite of it or of J-Block. Not sure which one.

J-Block was strictly MOB—money over broads. To him, females were good for only one thing. But you knew he was full of crap, especially since he was raised by his mother and grandmother. Obviously they were good for a little more than that. He did have two baby mamas—both of them were phat, light-skinned dimes. Neither of them could get his time unless they was talkin' business. Both posted up at Moe's faithfully like it was church, dragging snotty-nosed children behind them. It was probably the only chance they had to catch a glimpse of the man their children called Daddy, even though he never responded to the title.

"What up, kid," Trevor said to Rashid as he hopped into the passenger side of the Range.

"Oh, what up, Trevor, I didn't even see you," Rashid said.

"That's what I'm talking about, shorty." J-Block peeled off a fifty-dollar bill and handed it to Rashid. "You got me lookin' right." J-Block climbed into the driver's seat of the Range, got into a hustler lean, then peeled off heading up the busy block with Rashid's murderer. All eyes on them.

Rashid stashed the dough in the left pocket of his ripped jean shorts and then pulled out a twenty and a five and handed the money to me.

"Here, put this in our account." When we started working at Moe's, we made a pact to put half of our combined tips in an account for college. Hustlers paid well. At last count, we had about two Gs in the pot. We figured that the money would help cover two years for Rashid at community college and I would get a scholarship somewhere. Rashid wanted to be a lawyer and defend people who were wrongly accused. Fight for justice.

I was never rolling through Moe's again. But that wouldn't necessarily solve the problem of running into Trevor. East Baltimore ain't but so big.

eight

plain and simple

MY mother took it upon herself to go door to door and ask neighbors if anyone knew anything related to her son's murder. My father told her to wait for him to get off work, so that they could go together and he could be the reasonable one. But time was of the essence and my mother knew we didn't have much of it. So she dragged me with her.

Some neighbors voiced their agreement with the fact that something needed to change in the community, that we needed to stick together, but they still didn't know anything. Others gave short condolences and wished they knew something. The rest flat-out ignored her knocks like she was a Jehovah's Witness.

Then it was on to Ms. Rosalie's house. I was hoping Teeny was there so that I could talk to him, but she sent him to stay at his father's house for a little while.

"You know how much I loved Rashid and I wish there was something I could do," she said to my mother. Ms. Rosalie's eyes had huge rings around them and sadness covered her face. I felt bad for her. She didn't have a man like my father at home to protect her family. I looked at her and tried to let her know that I understood where she was coming from.

"You're sure Teeny doesn't know who did it?" my mother asked her friend for the fifth time.

"I'm sure," Ms. Rosalie said. But her face said it all. She couldn't look my mother in the eyes and she kept wiping her kitchen table with a cloth even though it was clean.

"I want justice, plain and simple," my mother said.

"We all do," Ms. Rosalie added, although we all knew justice was far from plain or simple.

"I just find it hard to believe that Teeny didn't see anything. He and Rashid are always together. He was at the courts that day and I know they always walked home together." My mother wouldn't let it go. Ms. Rosalie and Moms had been friends long enough for my mother to know that Ms. Rosalie wasn't being straight with her.

I started to feel real bad because I knew who killed

Rashid and couldn't find the courage to tell my mother. But that was because I was protecting our family. Maybe Ms. Rosalie was doing the same?

Ms. Rosalie looked away and peered through her window at two teenage girls arguing outside. She shook her head. "This neighborhood has changed," she commented.

"We have to take it back!" my mother half shouted. "We have to start with our own. Rashid was our son!" Both of them were crying by this point— an act that didn't really affect me. I had heard more of it in the last few days than I had in my entire life.

"I won't stop until I get justice, whether you help me or not," my mother said as we walked toward the door.

"Yvette, I will help you in any way I can," Rosalie pleaded. I knew she meant it.

My mother stared at Ms. Rosalie like she was looking into her soul for answers. When we got back into the car, she vowed to never see her friend again.

When we reached home, our feet blistered from pavement pounding, my mother turned her interrogations toward me. I was still in semi-shock and really didn't understand her questions. I answered no because it sounded right.

"Think!" she yelled at my numbness.

I knew that she felt bad for her harsh tone, but it

was like some strange spirit had taken over her body. My father stepped in to try to cool things down. "Son, don't be afraid. If you know who did this, just tell us." He rubbed my back. I wondered if my father had heard anything about Trevor. But if he did I'm sure he would do something. I guess?

I shrugged my shoulders and struggled to keep the tears from leaving my eyes. Tavon's voice echoed in my head. I wondered if my face gave me away.

My mother kept pleading, but my father told her to let it go. "Well, if you do hear something, you'll be sure to say something, right?"

I nodded my head yes to make them happy. Disgust bubbled in my stomach like bad food.

"I'm going to go lie down," I said. My mother shook her head with a new type of disappointment. My father told me to rest well.

I wish I could. I hadn't rested well since the last time I saw Rashid. Most of the time if I was in bed, I was thinking about something too serious for my young brain. Like what made Darryl punk Trevor, knowing that word would get back to Peety and crap would hit the fan. Darryl was forced to take a trip out of town for who knows how long. Fact is, Darryl ain't never been the sharpest tool in the shed. He was too hot-headed to work as muscle for any of the local dealers, although his size—six-five and two hundred and fifty pounds and do-or-die attitude would have made him fit for the role. Muscle still had to be calculating and efficient. Darryl was sloppy and impatient. Still, he took pleasure from handling cats and making them feel as little as they looked to him.

I thought about the scene I didn't witness, over and over again in my head. It was a chain of events that I wanted so badly to disrupt. I wanted Darryl to have shut the hell up. I wanted Rashid to have caught a cramp in his leg and be forced to stop playing and go home. Or I wanted Rashid to be standing two feet to the left so that he would have missed the nameless bullet. I wished Trevor would have just fought Darryl. Or I wished Trevor would have gotten hit by a car when he went to get the gun. I visualized everything else but what really happened.

nine

slow crying

NEW Saints was decorated with bundles of flowers in bright shades of yellow, red and purple—small efforts to bring life to the dead air that was floating through the church. It's true: You can tell how much a person has touched other people by his funeral. I doubt that means that just because someone has a crowded funeral that he was loved. But in Rashid's case, his life had meant something to almost everyone he had come in contact with. A few of his elementary school teachers who remembered his sense of humor and young wisdom came out. Cats from around the way who respected "lil' man" for not taking any crap, but also being clear that the game wasn't for him, showed up in shorts and Tims.

Most, if not all of New Saints' congregation attended to tell us that Rashid was in a better place. "It's just a shame," Sister Thomasina said. "He was a good boy. Not like those other hoodlums who cause so much trouble in our neighborhood."

The wake held earlier that morning was unbearable. Everyone kept telling my parents and me how sorry they were. Sorry? Sorry didn't mean much to me. I was glad that they came out to pay their respects, but why did they have to tell me they were sorry? Why did they have to say anything? I preferred silence—an unstated agreement that told me how they felt. I knew how they felt, but they had no idea how I felt. And I hated that they fronted like they did.

After a while, none of it sounded sincere anymore. Everyone just became shadows, blank figures with empty words. Resentment began to creep up my back.

"My condolences," one figure would say before moving on, leaving the church and going forward with life.

"Your family is in my prayers," another shadow would say while grabbing my hands. "This, too, shall pass," an elder would say, but wouldn't offer any information on when "this" would actually go away.

"Another one of our own has been taken too soon," said an elderly black woman who was hunched over a walker. "When will the madness end?" she pondered out loud to no one in particular.

As time passed, I couldn't hear anything. I saw people's mouths moving, but heard no sound. I craved the silence. I wanted more of it. I closed my eyes and enjoyed the darkness. Visions of Rashid alive, laughing, flashed like bright lights and lightened my pain. Extended family, friends and neighbors continued their sympathy wishes, but I ignored them. I tried desperately to float away to my own world.

The gathering of family and friends and their condolences didn't offer much comfort to my mother either. Patterson Heights may not have shown up at the police department looking for justice, but they did show up at the funeral to pay their respects. This made my mother sick to her stomach, but she lacked the energy to lash out like I knew she could. If she had the energy to speak for real, she would call them all hypocrites—accomplices in her son's murder. She died a second death at the standing-room-only ceremony. Rings took up permanent residence under her eyes. The hair that she had styled weekly at the beauty salon was a reddish brown pile on top of her head. I hated to see her look so crazy. Her mother, who didn't shed one tear for her grandson—she seemed more bothered that she had to come down from New

Jersey and miss her weekly tennis match—forced my mother to wear a hat. I was happy when grandma took her bourgie butt back home.

My uncle Brian, Moms' older brother, flew up from Jacksonville and helped her skeleton-like body down the aisle. Tavon's father, Uncle Darius, was on the other side. He cleaned himself up for just enough time to be at his nephew's funeral. We hardly ever saw him unless he needed money for his habit. But it was my mother who now looked like the junkie. She lost like five pounds in a week's time and had to go to the hospital because she was so tired it was affecting her health. "I don't have time to eat or sleep," she said while lying in the hospital bed. "I have to find my son's murderer." My heart dropped seeing her in pain and I knew I could help if I just confessed what I knew. I was so close to speaking up, but something, and I'm not sure what, stopped me.

My father stood strong. No tears. He handled the affairs of his son's funeral with a straight face. He sat by his wife's side during her hospital visit. He hugged me when I looked like I couldn't take it anymore. He took care of out-of-town family members. All the while he must have been on the brink of exploding.

The ceremony was a blur to me. I didn't cry. I wanted to but couldn't. I figured I had run out of tears. Deadness had attacked me from the moment I stepped into the church. I didn't fight it. How do you fight death?

Had I been fully conscious at the funeral I would have experienced a moving program. I would have heard people of all ages praise my brother. I would have heard words of encouragement to help me get through such a trying time. I would have heard Reverend Sullivan give a stirring sermon about God's plan for Rashid.

But I didn't hear any of it. And then it was over. People again told us how sorry they were. And then they left. Some gathered at our house to grub more food. Then they left, too. Eventually it was just the three, not four, of us.

"How are you, son?" my father asked after the last visitors left our house. Tortured. That's how I was doing. Like someone was punishing me for some terrible crime that I didn't commit.

My mother sat next to me on the living room sofa and grabbed my hand. She didn't look at me, though. It was like she was staring at nothing. Seeing something I couldn't see.

"I don't think everything has really hit me," I said.

"That's natural," he said. "Don't be afraid to come to your mother or I for anything. If you need to talk or vent or cry. It's okay. We're here for you."

My mother squeezed my hand and I squeezed back. That night my parents were talking in their room about Rashid. They tried not to talk about bad stuff dealing with my brother in front of me. They didn't do a good job of it.

"I never thought we would have to shell out thousands of dollars for our son's funeral," my father said. She didn't respond. Usually a control freak, my mother left all the funeral details to Pops—including what flowers would surround the church altar and what the program would say.

"I've always put money aside for us for a rainy day, but no one told me to save just in case we had to buy a box to house our son's body."

"What do you want me to do?" my mother asked with frustration in her voice. "You're yelling at me like I can do something."

"Honey," my father said in a much more calm voice. "I'm not yelling at you. I'm just venting. I need to get it out. I'm disgusted that people are actually in the business of celebrating death. Trying to talk us into a fancy coffin as if that's going to bring Rashid back."

"We should get the best for Rashid. He deserved it."

"I don't disagree with you. Our son deserved the best and we did a great job of giving him as much as we could. What I'm saying now is we don't have much to give. We have to make sure we have enough for us and Avery. Our credit cards are maxed out. I had to use most of the college fund that we just started to really save for."

I didn't hear my mother say anything. But I knew that it was killing my father that one of his sons wasn't going to reach his potential. That's all he would talk about when it came to Rashid and I. He knew all the numbers thrown around that suggested that his boys wouldn't make it. But he knew that Rashid and I had good heads on our shoulders. He had honest conversations with us; giving us real-world advice, not that in-denial crap. He told us about STDs and that if we were going to have sex, to always, always use a condom. He gave us information about what to do if we were arrested, so that we knew our legal rights. He admitted to us that he used to smoke weed when he was younger, but he didn't want us to make the same mistakes. He showed us how to treat women through the way he acted around our mother. He shunned "punks" like rappers who disrespected females. He told us that even if we didn't step foot in a church when we got older, we had to find a way to connect with a higher power. He didn't like fighting, but told us it was important to stand up for ourselves and our beliefs. He always talked about the importance of education and he had even begun taking night classes at Morgan State University to show us that it was never too late to accomplish a goal. He told us about the practical stuff, too—good hygiene, saving money, respecting one's elders and how to act like a gentleman.

He did all of this without a true example from his own parents. He never really got to know his father, CC, short for Cassius Carl, as the West Baltimore neighborhood used to call their local boxing champ, before cancer claimed his life at the young age of thirty-two. My father's mother died shortly after. As a young man, my father learned about survival as a child of the state.

He prided himself on overcoming odds and being a model of manhood for his sons—a responsible father and husband. Yeah, he knew what people said about Baltimore and he knew the murder rate was enough to make many avoid claiming the city as home. But he was faithful that Rashid and I would be okay.

"I am not blaming you," my father said to my mother. "I blame myself. I've scanned the seventeen years that Rashid was alive looking for the part where I missed something—the part when, as his father, I forgot to impart wisdom. I can't find that specific time, but I spend every available moment trying. Rashid died more than in vain. He died as a stereotypical cliché and I'm starting to hate myself for it." I heard Moms crying. Again. I knew it was all too much for her. But Dad was going through it, too.

I wanted to tell my father that it wasn't his fault. I waited for my mother to say it for me. She didn't.

If I could, I would have permanently closed my eyes to continue living in peace. Instead, that night I stopped talking. I figured that keeping my mouth shut was the best plan of action.

ten

watch your
tongue

A bright sun peered through my windows. I had
watched it emerge from its hiding place. I shifted in
my bed and tried to shield my eyes from the light. I
waited for a knock on the door from Rashid to tell
me it was my turn to hop in the shower. Nothing. I
waited for the smell of maple ham or hickory-smoked
bacon to creep into my room. There was nothing but
blaring silence. I wondered if I would have to iron
slacks and pick out a matching shirt. No one came
and told me to get dressed. For the first time I could
remember, my family was not going to church.

The red numbers on my digital alarm clock read

9:36. Service had already begun. I thought that one day I'd be relieved for this day—just to be able to sleep in. Maybe catch whatever came on television while we were sitting in the pews at New Saints. I grabbed the remote. Cable was a waste of money to Pops. So after flipping through only five channels that mainly featured a mixture of infomercials and boring political shows with a bunch of white men talking, I hit the Off button.

Alone with my thoughts again. Time: 9:43. I heard movement in the hallway. My parents were up. I thought that maybe they were going to attend the noon service instead. There was a knock on my door. I almost expected Rashid to be on the other end until I remembered.

I got up from the bed like an old head and opened it.

"Hey, son," my father said, still in pajamas. He hadn't shaved in a few days, so there was mad stubble on his face. His eyes were red like he didn't sleep well either.

Since my father didn't have on one of his church suits, I was partly glad to know that I wouldn't have to deal with the sympathetic wishes of everyone at New Saints. But seeing him not dressed also made me realize that things were different. The routine that my family once had was disturbed and might never return to what it once was. I was scared.

"Want to go to breakfast?" he asked. The idea of leaving the house made me nervous. I shook my head. Talking was no longer an option for me.

He asked me a few other questions that I can't remember. To all of them I responded through head nods and shoulder shrugs.

"Are you okay?" He gave me that concerned dad look. I shook my head up and down and walked back to my bed. He stood at the doorway trying to think of what to say next. After a few minutes he went away.

Later during the day, my parents realized that I wasn't talking. They were sitting on the couch reading all the cards we received at the funeral and in the mail, when my mother called me out of my room. My father was making a list of people who they had to send thank-you cards to. On the CD player some woman with a depressing voice sang about losing love.

They asked me to join them, to read some of the cards. I wasn't interested in reading pain on paper.

"Son, you haven't said anything all day. Is everything okay?" Pops asked. When I didn't verbally answer that question either, my parents both took long, deep breaths.

"If you're not going to talk, you still need to communicate with us using more than shrugs and nods," Moms said. I could tell she was worried. She was rubbing her hands back and forth to try to calm her nerves.

"It's okay, if not talking helps you through the grieving process," my father said. He shot my mother a strange look.

I stood in front of them for a few more minutes to make sure they were finished. When they didn't say anything else, I turned around and headed back to my room, the only place that felt bearable.

eleven

county blues

"BE careful with that," my mother shrieked. "It's the trophy from his middle school basketball championship."

She and I were packing Rashid's things. I sloppily wrapped a piece of the *Sun* around the plastic award. I was tempted to throw it into the box filled with other non-fragile stuff, but knew that would make my even-more-fragile mother explode.

It was the day before moving day. Moms was convinced that the neighborhood we had lived in since Rashid and I were born was now an evil wasteland of death and destruction. Forget the fact that Rashid wasn't actually killed in Patterson Heights, but five blocks over in what was considered Masey Square.

That didn't matter to her. She wanted to be as far away as possible from the memory that was slowly killing her. If we had the money, she'd probably try to relocate to some deserted farm in Nowhere, USA. She settled for the County. I wouldn't have admitted it, but I was a little shook to still be living around the way knowing that Peety was involved in things. But leaving my neighborhood never popped into my head.

My mother also wanted to sell our house. At that point, even I knew she was tripping. My parents purchased it before Rashid was born and they were determined to pass it down to us. It was something they knew rich people did with their kids.

Pops didn't feel the move was necessary. He thought it was the opposite, plus expensive. He and my mother had already had an argument over the fact that she wanted to move into a three-bedroom apartment so that she could still keep Rashid's stuff in a separate room. But even with one less son, he wasn't about to waste money. He put his foot down. "We can move," he told her, "but only into a two-bedroom apartment." All of Rashid's stuff would occupy my room. Pops also said that things would be real tight because he would have to pay rent at the new spot and the mortgage at our old house until he found people to rent it.

The County might as well have been outer space to

me, the unknown. Most cats talked trash about it. The County was soft, they'd say. Other cats made it out to be some fantasy place with prettier girls and bigger houses, placing it on some diamond-encrusted pedestal. As if the moment you changed zip codes, you automatically became somebody better. I didn't buy into all of that.

It was true. Patterson Heights had a reputation for handling business. When I told people that I was from The Heights, respect was automatically paid. My family's street was real. Real in the sense that real people with real problems lived on it. The sidewalks told stories when you traveled them—stories of life situations when sometimes ends don't meet or things weren't always pretty or perfect. But those sidewalks also told tales of birthday celebrations and block parties, job promotions and proud parents sending their children to college. Patterson Heights was balanced. For every killing, there was someone who survived and became somebody. For every young hustler, there was a kid who worked legit. For every single mother, there was a family like mine. It was a great place to grow up, to live—until everything changed.

As I wrapped my brother's stuff, I wondered, how do you leave a place that you've known your entire life? The only place you've lived? The place where you learned how to ride a bike and kiss a girl? How do you leave it all behind and act like it never meant anything?

My parents didn't bother to find out how I felt about the move. Pops did say this: "You know you can always come back around the way with me when I visit Ronald and all of them." Translation: I wasn't to step foot back in the old neighborhood without supervision. The chances that my father would go back in the near future were slim to none.

We were moving on without moving on.

Lakewood Gardens, "a tranquil community nestled in the heart of Baltimore County" as the brochure read, was a mixture of black and white families looking to move on up—an apartment complex that didn't possess a lake, gardens or woods. Just mad trees—a fact that excited my mother, like the presence of bark, branches and leaves meant protection. Now that we had pines in our neighborhood, our family would be safe from the cold, cold world. I was never a tree hugger and had no intentions of becoming one. That didn't matter. My mother was hell-bent on keeping me on lockdown. Even in the quiet County.

We downgraded. We went from a three-level house into a tight but more expensive apartment with only two rather small bedrooms. And it smelled funny, like wet animals. The entire place had this ugly brown carpet, which because we never had it in our other house, felt weird under my feet.

"It's kind of exciting. It's like we're getting a new start," my father said as he moved boxes around. He was fronting. He didn't want to leave either. I just shrugged my shoulders.

New home also meant new school. I was glad that I wouldn't have to show up any longer at Central—too many memories there. Rashid would have been a senior. That following year, according to our plan, he was supposed to enroll in Maryland Community College and get his grades up, so that we could attend a four-year institution together. Without Rashid, the idea of going to school to achieve our goal didn't seem right to me. But I knew I didn't have a choice in the matter. Dropping out was not an option in my household.

But I didn't want to go to some bourgie County school either. My mother fought with a few administrators to get me enrolled in Macon Academy and she expected me to be grateful. The name alone sounded corny. I imagined brothers rocking tight khakis, striped socks and button-downs that were tucked in. The chicks would probably want dudes with expensive rides to take them to Charleston Mall, the ritzy shopping mecca of the County. Not a good look for broke dudes.

Summer would retire in two weeks. I didn't bother trying to meet people in the new neighborhood or explore my new environment. I hibernated for the remainder of the time, only getting out of bed to eat and use the restroom, or when my parents forced me—all without talking.

twelve

A mother scorned

MY mother turned pain into obsession over finding Rashid's killer. She didn't accept "we're working all leads" as an answer to her inquiries. She needed to know how, what, when, where and why. Pops told her to fall back and let the professionals do their job. But she was convinced that the officers didn't automatically care about the death of another black boy. She had to make them care.

She took up part-time residence on the hard wooden bench at police headquarters downtown. She told my father she was using up her vacation days from work. He didn't have any left. So on some days when I think she was lonely, she forced me out of my sleep and dragged me with her.

Headquarters didn't look anything like police stations do on television. No loud, ringing phones or arguing suspects. It was busy, just not a circus. You would think that Baltimore was mad safe with how quiet police central was. There were other people like my mother and I trying to get answers and usually families like ours gave the place some life.

That day my mother brought her iPod which only housed what she called "the classics"—folks like Nina Simone, Stevie Wonder and Earth, Wind & Fire. Their souls calmed her own. She deleted her gospel collection. I brought nothing. I just sat there, zoned out, slept or I watched the folks that came in and out. Some of their faces were heavy with stories, so I began to read them to pass the time. One woman's spoke sadness. She was wearing a tight silver halter top, showing her belly, which looked like it had already popped out a few kids. Her short skirt revealed bruised thighs. But she looked like she was still a little girl, just dressed like a woman.

After a while, I read some of the pamphlets in the waiting area. One was on reporting illegal guns as a way to help stop murders. It was a good idea, but I knew it probably didn't work. Another was about an anonymous line that you could call to report crime. For a minute, I thought it could be my solution. I could just call the number and everything would go back to normal. Then I heard my cousin Tavon's voice telling me not to trust it. I put the pamphlet back.

By midafternoon, my mother began telling me stories about Rashid. Like when he was twelve years old, he told her that if he didn't get accepted into college, he'd enroll in the police academy. "I'm gonna lock up all the bad people," he told her one day after school. He always had a plan B.

My mother also told me that the day Rashid was born was one of the happiest days of her life. Even happier than the quiet wedding she and my dad shared. The short ceremony was followed by a cook-out. She said she was so in love that she didn't need all the fancy stuff to prove it.

"Rashid was the first manifestation of that love," she said, staring into space. "I loved him at first sight. From the moment the nurse placed him in my arms, I vowed to cherish and protect him. I've only made good on one of my two promises." She was about to continue, but she saw Detective Sanders, the officer on Rashid's case. He was a short white man who had more hair on his face than on his head. When the murder first happened, he came to our house to talk to us. He called my brother's case "typical." Black kid, shot near a basketball court, probably over some neighborhood beef. My father was quick to dig into him and let him know that Rashid wasn't just some kid and that he wasn't involved in the streets. "I'll make a note of that," the detective said.

"Detective Sanders, can I have a moment of your time?" He rolled his eyes at my mother and then took a deep breath. She asked him if he had any more information. "I told you, Mrs. Washington, if there are any new developments, you will be the first to know." He pushed the few strands on the top of his head to the left.

That wasn't good enough. My mother pressed him to find out what they were doing. She demanded details. She provided him with the names of neighbors to question again. Then she flashed baby pictures of Rashid, old report cards and photos of him at the junior prom to remind Detective Sanders what was important.

None of it seemed to work. "Look, the more you bother me, the less time I have to devote to your son's case. We're investigating all leads." He tucked his oversized white cotton shirt into his undersized khaki pants. He was sweating like he had just run ball. There were green rings under the arms of his shirt. We could smell both his bad hygiene and the onions he must have just eaten.

"But my son's murderer is walking the streets. Doesn't that mean anything to you?" Her voice was now a shout, which must be a natural occurrence at headquarters. No one was bothered by her outburst.

It was like her voice was useless, no matter how high or loud she raised it.

"It doesn't matter if it means anything to me," he said with an attitude. "I've been on the force for seventeen years. And I started out as one of those gung-ho cops who got a real sense of accomplishment from fighting crime and throwing bad guys in jail. But all that time makes you disillusioned. I've seen savvy criminals get off on legal loopholes, fellow officers abuse their authority and families like yours not get the justice they deserve. Every day, I risk my life for people I don't know or who probably don't care if I drop dead tomorrow. So pardon me if I'm not as emotional as you think I should be. All I can tell you is that we're working leads. We're doing our jobs. But beyond that, I have nothing more to give. Now if you excuse me, I have ten unsolved murders to get back to."

We watched Detective Sanders walk away. Then we turned around and left feeling defeated.

thirteen

school Daze

MY mother didn't want me walking to school on my first day. Too dangerous. She fought with my father over the issue during breakfast. Well, it wasn't really breakfast. I was sitting at the table eating Cheerios without milk. We had run out and my mother, who usually did the grocery shopping, hadn't bothered to cop some more. She was scanning the newspaper looking for any info about Rashid's case, which really didn't make sense to me. She had on her new uniform: sweatpants with a sweatshirt wrapped around her waist, T-shirt and sneakers. Pops was grabbing a cup of coffee and buttoning his United States Postal Service shirt.

"It's only a few blocks away," he said.

"And? The courts were only a few blocks away. What does distance have to do with anything?" Every opportunity she got, my mother seemed to bring up Rashid.

He stopped at the last button and rubbed his forehead. My father already felt bad and her comments only added to the mounting guilt he was fighting. I knew the feeling. And as the man of the household, my father thought he should have been there to protect Rashid. To take the bullet himself if need be. That's what fathers did and mine felt like he failed.

"We can't protect Avery every second of the day," he said. "We can only do our best and have faith that he will be okay."

"Faith? Are you talking about the same faith that I had when Rashid walked out our door and never came back, that faith?" My mother slammed the newspaper on the table. It didn't make a big sound.

My father didn't answer her. He was talking about that faith, but he knew she no longer believed in it. And I think he was worried that he didn't either.

So he agreed to drive me to school on my first day.

The car was quiet except for the constant swipe of the windshield wipers. It was drizzling in Baltimore. My father hated that. He figured if it should rain, let it pour, not half-ass it.

He and I hadn't spent much time together in the

last month. He asked me how I was doing, I guess hoping that I would answer. I didn't. But he kept talking.

"So did you sleep well last night?" Pops asked.

I never looked up. If I had, my father would have seen the bags under my eyes. I had hardly slept in weeks.

"I think I'm going to go ahead and get cable, so we can keep up on sports. How's that sound?"

I shrugged my shoulders. I knew we couldn't afford it and my father knew I wasn't the one into sports. That was Rashid.

"You ever thought about trying out for a team, now that you're a big sophomore and all?"

This time I didn't bother to shrug my shoulders, nod my head or answer with my hands. Instead I stared at the small raindrops that hit the window. I watched how they slowly slid down the glass and lost their shape, their being. I felt myself doing the same thing.

I was tired and not just from lack of sleep. It required too much energy to act like everything was okay.

My father stopped trying and we rode in silence.

Macon Academy used to be Macon High School until some brilliant administrator thought changing the name was an easy way to enhance the school's image. He was half-right. Most folks continued to call it by the old name and the school didn't manage to become any better as a result. It still dished out below-decent educations to a bulk of the student body. But to strangers unfamiliar with the school, it was able to front like it was a high-class place.

Outside, the school sported a big white sign that was surrounded by a bright-ass green lawn that looked like it had just been cut. That was just another front. Inside, the school mirrored one of those ancient jails—nothing about its dark interior excited students about learning; just the opposite. It was a dump. I couldn't figure out why my parents wanted me to go so badly.

The kids didn't look so much different than they did at Central. There were still cliques: the cute girls, the pretty boys, the jocks, the weirdos. I never had to be a part of a clique before because Rashid was cool with everyone. In the cafeteria on any given day, he would be talking game with the basketball players, hollering at the pretty girls or learning something new from the weirdos. I was always right with him.

Now I had to try to define myself. Find out where I fit in. I looked around and the answer was nowhere. I was destined to be alone.

Usually Rashid and I would hit up the mall to cop new gear for the first weeks of school. My father offered to take me shopping, but I wasn't feeling it. I'd rather rock something of my brother's because for some reason, I thought it would make the day go a little easier. That morning, I grabbed one of Rashid's favorite basketball jerseys to go with my black jeans—my small frame couldn't fill my brother's pants.

I looked down at the class schedule that was mailed to my house. Moms made sure I was enrolled in the advanced placement classes, but I didn't want to exceed. I just wanted to drift—in and out of reality.

Rashid was always shooting compliments at me for being smart even though some cats around the way didn't respect a row of As on a report card. "Yo, intelligence is the key to doing big things," he'd always tell me. "Dudes around here are stupid for thinking that stupid is something to be proud of." I let Rashid's words give me strength.

When I reached homeroom, I grabbed a seat in the back, hoping to go unnoticed—which worked as best to be expected. Most of the guys who staggered into the classroom peeped me but didn't speak. The girls gave me the once-over but kept it moving. Before the bell rang, everyone but me chatted about their summers and who they saw in the hallways during the trip to homeroom.

I didn't pay much attention to them. I didn't check out who was cute. I didn't compare my clothes to my male competition. Instead, I kept my eyes glued to the metal desk where I sat. The name "Keyshawn" graced the top. A school custodian probably scraped hard to rid the desk of the vandalism, but the permanent marker remained. I desired that type of power, to remain despite what life threw at me.

"Avery Washington," Mrs. Pain called. It took a moment for me to snap out of my thoughts. I raised my hand. She told me to come to her desk.

As I walked up the aisle, I could feel my classmates' eyes stuck on me. I heard whispers about my newness. I heard cats wondering where I was from. But I kept walking because I knew if I stopped, I might not start again.

"Your parents told me of your situation," Mrs. Pain said in a low voice like she was discussing some embarrassing problem.

She was a chunky woman who bulged out of her cheap-looking black suit. But her face was genuine as she spoke. "I will do all I can to accommodate you."

I nodded my head and returned to my desk the same way I came.

The rest of my classes were like that. I would daydream, and something, usually the mention of my name, would knock me out of my world.

My first day at Macon Academy was uneventful— the way I wanted it. I made it through without uttering a word. I didn't have to be friendly—kids just automatically pegged me as weird. I was fine with that.

My mother waited promptly for me in the parking lot when school was over. I opened the door and was about to hop in, but in the passenger seat there were tons of fliers with Rashid's face. I was thrown off when I saw my brother staring back at me. I grabbed the batch and covered them with my book bag.

Moms smelled like she forgot to put on deodorant that morning. The gray T-shirt she wore was stuck to her back by sweat.

"So how was it?" I could tell my mother hoped that I would answer using words. Instead I made a gesture with my hands that let her know it was fine.

She looked too tired to press me. She had spent her morning—after taking the day off work again—plastering fliers around the old neighborhood trying to get someone, anyone, to step forward with a tip about the murder.

fourteen

it ain't where you from

FOr the most part, my first week at Macon went like the first day. I just showed up, which I felt was more than enough. Not talking was easier than I imagined it would be. Most of my teachers respected my need to be mute—probably because it was one less kid talking out of turn in class. I wasn't talked to either. Nor was I bothered.

Until cats thought it was time to test me—see how much I was repping Patterson Heights.

It started with a shoulder shove. I thought it was an accident and kept it moving. The shove was followed by, "'cuse you." I didn't think I was the one being addressed, so I kept it moving. The "'cuse you" was followed by, "Yo, don't you hear me talking to you?" That's when I knew that I was the one being spoken to. Although I didn't want to, I turned around.

I had been in only two fights in my life, and both times, Rashid was by my side throwing blows.

The dude who shoved me was a head smaller than me, although his 'fro gave him a little height. He was built like a miniwrestler and had a discoloration around his eye that made him look like he was wearing a patch. I couldn't help but stare at it.

"What you looking at?" the little man asked aggressively.

I remained silent. I wasn't going to break my peace for a fool trying to cook beef in front of me. I turned around and started toward my next class.

Eye patch took that as disrespect. He charged behind me and punched me in the back of the neck. Hard. Little man knocked me down. A bigger crowd formed. All wanted to see how the new kid from The Heights was going to retaliate. They wanted a brawl. But I knew firsthand how beef could go from a few choice words to bullets to the chest. I caught my breath. Little man knocked the wind out of me. I sat up, but didn't get up.

Taunts circled me.

"Damn, Billy knocked you down with one punch."

"Yo he ain't from The Heights, he frontin'."

"Not unless he got smacked up every day," a spectator said before exchanging pounds with another onlooker.

"He don't want any more of this," my attacker said before picking up his books and strolling away from the crowd like a fake gangster.

I disappointed them. I had no desire to rumble with little man. The crowd eventually got bored and bounced, leaving me on the floor with my pride next to me.

During lunch, I sat alone, a state that started to feel natural, although deep down, I was lonely. But I wasn't as ashamed of myself as my schoolmates seemed to be. Cats walked past me either laughing or shaking their heads. I figured it would blow over, and if not, I really didn't care. So what I was pushed to the ground. My brother was below it.

When I looked up from my rubbery pizza, a kid rocking a pink polo shirt with the collar up, designer sunglasses and pink and white Nikes was staring at me.

"What up?" the pretty boy said.

I gave him a head nod and continued picking off the pepperonis.

"Yo, why you go out like that earlier?" pretty boy asked like he and I were cool like that.

I offered a smirk. Not because I thought something was funny, but because I couldn't believe how caught up everyone was over dumb stuff.

"What, you don't speak?"

I wanted to say, "Yeah, fool, I don't," but of course that would defeat my vow of silence.

Pretty boy dropped his pink backpack on the table and plopped into a seat. I looked around to see if this was some kind of game people played on the new kid.

"You a mute?"

I started to mean-mug slim. Rashid used to always tell me that I didn't really have an intimidating face. I wasn't surprised that it didn't work. Pretty boy started talking again.

"You don't dress like a city cat." He examined my clothes. He sounded like a cross between a dirty south rapper and a college professor. One of the accents didn't fit. Slim was definitely trying too hard.

"You probably could have taken Billy. Why you punk out? It was like you didn't care."

I wondered how long pretty boy would talk without a response. I could tell that slim was the selfish type since he didn't seem at all interested in carrying a conversation. He just wanted to hear his own voice.

"By the way, I'm Ricardo, but around here they call me Pretty Ricky," he laughed at himself. I was growing more annoyed and looked at my watch to see when lunch would be over. Six minutes.

While Ricardo kept talking about himself, which included a discussion about the girls he was going to hook up with during the school year, the new gear he copped and was planning to show off, as well as how he was getting down with some crew who "ran shit," I started to visualize my schoolmates as faceless shadows who lacked hearts and souls. They floated around the colorful metal chairs worried about meaningless crap.

The bell rang and I jumped up, leaving Pretty Ricky talking to himself.

"Yo, I'll catch you later." I heard him yell out. I didn't turn around.

When I got home from grinding through my first week at a school made up of wannabe thugs, stuck-up chicks and self-centered shadows, my parents were eager to hear how things went. They thought being around new young people would cure my silence. When I didn't answer any of their questions verbally, but instead used my head to provide yes and no nods, my parents were frozen with frustration, clueless as to how to proceed.

So they blamed each other and fought through the night. No one ever won these arguments and they never really made up afterward. Instead, the mean words started to cut through the foundation of their once-loving relationship.

I tried to shut out the loud voices. My pillow didn't work. The iPod I'd shared with Rashid was dead and I couldn't find the charger. So I opted for sleep, which was really a struggle. When I finally drifted away, I dreamed of shadowy figures who communicated only through high-pitched screams.

fifteen

breathe easy

Leaving Baltimore and staying with my uncle in Virginia after the shooting was good for me. For one, my uncle Anthony wasn't in the drug game. He didn't have the stomach for it, but he did have the balls to tell Peety that. Instead, Anthony managed some of my dad's real estate properties down south. He preferred a quieter, nonviolent life.

Anthony lived on a farm. At least, that's what it looked like to me. There was land for days, lots of trees and animals. Not farm animals, but I would spot the occasional skunk or deer. It was mad country, but I actually liked it. I could breathe and didn't have to watch my back. No one knew who

Trevor was and I wasn't constantly being given updates on who got shot or locked up.

When Anthony first found out that I was into art, he took me to the local library, where an illustrator was giving a talk about painting. I had never met anyone who did art for a living. I knew they existed, because how else did paintings get into art museums? But meeting an artist who made money from his work and being able to talk to the illustrator made me believe that following my love of drawing could really happen for me. I spent the majority of my time in Virginia being an artist. At least, that's how I liked to think about it.

There was a pond a short walk from my uncle's house. It was as close to paradise as I had ever seen or felt. I bought a sketchbook from the local Target and started drawing everything I saw, including a family of ducks and the large trees that provided shade.

When I was taking a break from being an artist, I was consuming words at the brain, my nickname for the library. I was never one who really liked sitting around with my face in a book. Or at least that's what I thought until I read something that interested me. It started with Donald Goines. Some of the stories were a little out of date, but I could get with the street side of the books. The tales of murder, drugs and betrayal reminded me of home. But after a while I was tired of being reminded of home. I wanted more—to be swept away to another world. That's when I discovered graphic novels—which combined the two things I liked: drawing and fantasy. The local library didn't have tons of them, so my uncle started ordering them online from a Web site that sold books. I rushed to the mailbox or the porch every day like I was waiting for a paycheck. I read ones about imaginary worlds, political figures like Nat Turner and Malcolm X, and about warriors with purpose. I thought about trying to draw and write my own, but the word part intimidated me.

I liked the person I was when I wasn't home, when I didn't have to represent. But all that didn't matter. Whenever Peety called, I always fronted like I was itching to get back to B'more and run shit.

sixteen

JUSTICE AIN'T FREE

GUN violence in Baltimore is as much a part of the city as steamed crabs. Murder is as common as Orioles and Ravens games. Responding to a reporter with a microphone in his face asking about a recent killing, a shop owner might say something like, "Someone got shot last night? Tell me something I don't know."

The reason why crime seemed to hit Baltimore like a tsunami is because it's really not that large. If the city had the size and population of a place like New York, its annual murder rate might not seem so deadly. But Baltimore ain't very big. You can get anywhere in the city in less than twenty minutes.

Plus it would be easier to ignore the statistics if

they weren't attached to real families. Politicians say that as long as you're not involved with the drug trade you're probably not going to be gunned down. They can't tell that to my mother though. She knew better; she learned otherwise.

Baltimore let her down: The cops who couldn't press charges. The courts who wouldn't do anything without any charges pressed. The neighbors who kept their mouths shut because of fear and the need to abide by a messed-up street code. Me.

My mother was forced to use most of her time trying to bring justice.

One night while I was watching repeats of *Law & Order,* Pops stormed out of my parents' room and left the house without any explanation. My mother yelled out, "See, you don't care. Go ahead, walk away."

I went to their room to see if she was okay. She was sitting on the edge of the bed with her head in her hands. Clothes were everywhere. Dishes were piled up on their dresser. I had never seen my parents' room like that. When she heard me enter, I didn't have to do anything to get her talking. She lifted her head completely. Sat up straight and began.

"I guess you should know now. I quit my job at Social Security so I can devote all my time to ensuring that Rashid's murderer ends up behind bars. Your father disagrees with my decision. I didn't do this for me. I did this for our family. We'll never be whole again until justice is served."

I felt torn between two crazy forces. I could understand why my mother felt justice was important. Maybe I was the barrier to it. But I could also see why Pops would be upset. Money was always tight for us and now there would be even less of it. Stuff was falling apart. And I was falling with it.

That next day, my mother set up a mobile office— a bunch of equipment and supplies that she purchased from the local Staples. She taught herself how to use a scanner so she could make Rashid's fliers herself. Using Excel, she created a database of all the local politicians she was going to contact about the case. She kept records of all the dealings with the police.

When my father got home from work, he didn't say anything about the expensive machinery that took up the dining room table. He was exhausted from pulling a few double shifts this week.

"Are you coming to the candlelight vigil?" she asked my dad while she typed like a mad woman on her new laptop. Since Rashid's death, my mother organized a weekly remembrance. I wasn't exactly sure what the point was of us standing outside with candles. Especially since we weren't doing it in the old neighborhood but outside some park my mother had randomly chosen. At first it was a lot of people, but each week there were less and less.

I was already dressed in slacks and a button-down and waiting in the recliner. For some reason, my mother thought that church clothes were appropriate.

"I'm tired," Pops said midyawn. He plopped on the couch and unbuttoned his blue shirt. The television remote was in one hand and the *Sun* in another.

"Tired?" she asked in disbelief. My father didn't respond.

"I'm talking to you," she said in a tone that she would use with me and Rashid, but never toward my father. I could tell he wasn't feeling it. He shifted in his seat and threw the remote onto the coffee table.

"Not with that attitude you're not," he shot back.

I wanted to walk back to my room, shut the door and try to zone out. But I knew my mother didn't want me going anywhere.

"So sitting on your tail watching reruns is more important than respecting your son's life?"

"You're so dramatic. I'm tired—nothing more, nothing less. This isn't about Rashid. This is about you wanting to control everything."

"No, you're trying to make it about me. This is about Rashid and paying respect to him." My mother dressed up only when we went to the vigil or to the graveyard. She had on a black dress that my father loved.

"You don't think I think about Rashid every day? I don't need to light a candle to remind me that I miss my son." My dad's eyes started to water. "I've pulled doubles almost every day this week trying to keep up with our bills, paying the mortgage at our house and trying to afford this new apartment that you had to have in the County." His forehead bulged. He took a deep breath and wiped his face with both hands. "You've got to give this up and let the cops do their jobs," he continued.

"This? This? Would you listen to yourself? You're telling me to give up on our son, to forget him."

"I am not saying that and you know it. I would never tell you to give up on Rashid. I'm sick and tired of you acting like you're the only one who has lost a son. He was my son, too."

"Well, it seems like I'm the only one who cares. I'm the one at the police department inquiring about progress in the case. I'm the one trying to get anyone to talk about what they saw that night. Me. Not you. Me!"

"Well, maybe I would have time to devote to the investigation if I didn't have to work like a dog to support this family."

"Now you're complaining because you have to support the family?" She sucked her teeth.

"I don't have a problem doing that, but we used

to be a team. What happened to us being a team? Now it feels like we're opponents."

"I can't tell. You walk around here like business as usual." My mother was hysterical.

"That's because if I don't, we would lose everything—the house, my job. I'm trying to keep this family together and make sure we don't become homeless after all of this. The funeral took a big chunk of our savings. We have hardly any left for a rainy day. I'm trying to ensure that we can keep moving. You think Rashid would want us to become homeless because we were too busy lighting candles instead of handling our business?"

My mother ran into the bedroom and slammed the door.

I sat quietly. There was no vigil that night.

silence is golden

"He won't talk," my mother told the disinterested receptionist at the HMO health center. I sat with my hood over my head, elbows on my legs and hands on my face. I was bored.

The medical facility was blindingly white, except for the stained gray carpet. The patients made Baltimore look like it was mad diverse. An Asian man rubbed his pregnant wife's belly. A few older white ladies were scattered around, all reading different women's magazines. A black man tried to keep his two toddler boys from running all over the place.

And then there was my mother and I. She had on the same sweats and T-shirt that she rocked the other day. A baseball cap covered her wild hair. Fashion, better yet, appearance, was no longer important. Tennis shoes were much more comfortable to wear as she walked the city looking for answers or harassing detectives at the police station.

During our twenty-five-minute wait, my mother asked the receptionist four times when we would be seen. Every time, she received the same answer from the blank-faced young woman: "When the doctor is ready to see you." Moms found this response unacceptable. But all of her attempts to intimidate the receptionist didn't make our wait time any shorter.

I would have usually been embarrassed by the way she was acting. But one, my mother wouldn't act like this under normal circumstances. Secondly, I didn't have much energy to devote to being embarrassed. I learned that after being knocked down on my first week of school and not feeling the urge to hide my face while walking the halls.

"Avery Washington," the receptionist called as she rolled her blue-contact eyes at my mother.

"Well, it took only twenty-seven minutes," my mother said as she threw up her hands. We followed the nurse into the back.

The doctor was even less interested in my problem than the receptionist. He looked like he should have been one of those male models. His face was perfect in a plastic sort of way. After checking my throat and neck glands, he said, "I suggest you take him to see a mental health professional. I'll provide a referral."

"He's not crazy," my mother replied.

"I didn't say he was, but the reason he is not talking has to do with his mind, not his body." The doctor kept clicking his pen like he was making a beat. I wanted to stick it down his throat. The sound was driving me crazy.

"Fine." I could tell my mother wanted to dig into him, but she didn't. She rushed me out of the small examination room, ripped the referral out of the receptionist's hand and headed out of the door.

"Do you need to see a shrink?" she asked.

I shrugged my shoulders. I had no idea. She tore up the referral and threw it into the wire trash can outside the office building.

"The doctor thinks our son needs to see a shrink," my mother reported to Dad when we got home. She was heating up a can of beans with pork chunks, a meal I hated.

"Doesn't sound like that could hurt," he responded.

I was irritated that my parents were talking like I wasn't in the room. They had been doing that a lot lately.

"Sometimes I think it's a good idea."

"What?"

"Silence."

"You think it's good that our son isn't talking?" My mother stopped stirring the beans and turned to my father. She folded her arms over her chest.

"I wish I could stop talking for a few days. Stop discussing what happened to our son. Stop answering questions from coworkers about how I am doing. Stop telling both of you that everything would be okay when I'm not quite sure myself. Stop arguing with you." He looked at my mother, then continued. "With silence comes clarity. Our son is probably just searching for understanding. Something we all need if we're going to survive."

For the first time in a long while, my mother had no comeback. Her eyes didn't look as hard as they had been. She listened to my father and I think she actually heard him.

eighteen

straighten it out

One Saturday morning, while I was chilling on the couch flipping channels, my mother called me into the kitchen. "Read this," she said, then handed me a section of the *Afro*. On the front page was one of Aunt Doreen's articles. When Rashid was murdered, my mother asked Doreen Harris, her friend from childhood and editor at the paper, to write a piece on the tragedy. Aunt Doreen covered the murder with care, and used Rashid's death, a child she thought of as one of her own, as a basis for a series of articles about black youth being in danger.

The article was about this program for youth called Straighten It Out that was led by some head doctor. It was supposed to allow young people to talk about issues that we were dealing with. "Our young people need safe spaces to express themselves, including their emotions," said Dr. McKenzie—the woman in charge of the program—in the article. "Many of them are dealing with heavy issues—that even adults struggle with—so it's important that we start imparting to them the skills they need to deal with the obstacles of life."

"I'm going to find out more about it," my mother said. That meant if she liked what she heard, I'd be enrolling. As far as my mother was concerned, if it wasn't featured in the *Afro,* it didn't happen. She was a faithful subscriber and believed that black newspapers were important to the community. It was a respect that she got from my grandfather who thought newspapers marked the sign of important people. And that's why he had tons of them in his house—issues from way back in the day—even though he couldn't read that well.

She called Aunt Doreen to see what she thought of the program. I could hear her over the phone. Aunt Doreen always talked like she was at a loud concert. She said that she thought the program was good because it gave young people something to do on Friday nights and because it had a positive mission to empower and educate teens.

When that Friday rolled around, my mother told me to get dressed and then she dropped me off. She told me she'd be back promptly in ninety minutes to pick me up. Once again change hit me upside the head.

Straighten It Out was held in a small, hot-ass basement of a small Baptist church on the Westside of the County about fifteen minutes from where we lived. The floor was covered by a sheet of dirt that looked like it had gotten comfortable. A rusty piano sat in one corner and a makeshift wooden stage stood for dear life at the back of the room. I remembered from the article that the group was temporarily meeting there. Apparently, a new facility was being built thanks to a grant from the city that Dr. McKenzie fought for after running the program for four years on a crazy small budget.

More new people, I thought as I dragged myself into the room. I was tired of being around strangers who thought they knew everything about me without knowing a thing. The twenty or so kids who were laughing, joking and giving one another hugs, immediately seemed real cliquish. I rolled my eyes tightly, took a deep breath and headed straight for the refreshments—incognito. It didn't work.

"Hi, you're new!" A cheery chick with thick glasses and big hoop earrings intersected me. Her hair was in a high ponytail that sat uncomfortably on the top of her head. She was average-looking.

"My name is Ramona," she said as she extended her hand.

I returned the gesture and shook her hand without introducing myself. Then I continued on my journey to the imitation Oreo cookies and punch. Ramona said something about me having an attitude, but I kept walking.

I studied the cookies, trying to determine how many to take. After spending nearly ten minutes paying too much attention to the small snack spread, I grabbed a seat outside of the circle of chairs where the rest of the group sat.

"Why are you sitting there?" a Puerto Rican–looking kid rocking a Yankees cap asked me. I provided my usual nonverbal answer.

"Suit yourself," the kid replied.

If I paid attention to my surroundings, I would have noticed that the group was split almost equally by males and females. I would have noticed that most of the kids were black with a few Latinos sprinkled in. I would have noticed that a handful of the girls were cuties of all types—long-haired, Rihanna short cuts and even some braids—and that the guys sported everything from the latest in Sean John to no-name sweats and tees. I would have heard accents from both East and West Baltimore.

But all I saw were more new people.

"What's up, crew?" Dr. McKenzie addressed the group energetically. She was fine. I mean like Beyoncé fine. You could tell she was old, probably like forty-something, but she wasn't all fat or out of shape like some women that age. I figured she must have worked out like every day and probably was one of those who didn't eat meat.

"What up, Doc?" one dude said louder than anyone else.

"Robin, those jeans are like that, where'd you get 'em?" Ramona asked Dr. McKenzie. Some of the other girls agreed.

"You like these? I got them from Macy's." She smiled. "Before we get started, I just wanted to remind you of a few things." She ran down some announcements about events around Baltimore that were "teen-friendly" as she put it and she talked about scheduling one-on-one time with her.

"Now who's going to get us started?" Three people raised their hands. They decided among themselves who would begin the session. Then, each kid in the group discussed one good thing that happened during the week and one challenge that they faced. The Puerto Rican–looking kid said that he started looking into local colleges, so he was excited about that. His challenge was staying sober and not getting drunk, something he said he fought every day. The Ramona girl said she got an A on a math test and her challenge was obeying her parents' rules. One kid talked about being treated bad by his father since he told him that he was gay. Another girl talked about the temptation to join a gang. The whole room had issues—some more serious than others. Dr. McKenzie would ask them questions and give them advice.

After the last kid in the circle was finished sharing, the group turned around and looked at me to participate. I saw Dr. McKenzie shake her head, her back-length hair followed. They took the hint and left me alone. Moms must have given her the heads up.

The second half of the night was devoted to violence. Dr. McKenzie showed a short documentary that explored different types of violence—wars, gang fights, domestic abuse and police brutality. Afterward, she asked the group to think about a time when they encountered violence and how they dealt with it.

I started to feel hot like I was staring into an oven. I wished that I had a bucket of water to splash on myself to cool off. Before Rashid, I wasn't really affected by seeing cats waving guns on television or the killings on those crime dramas that come on television. But murder had hit home and seeing lives treated like they didn't matter made me boil inside.

Oscar, I learned that was the Puerto Rican–looking kid's name, stood up and started talking first. He was a skinny kid with a head the size of a party balloon. He lived in a group home not far from the church.

"He just shot her." Oscar retold a story about

when he watched his father shoot his mother. He told the story like it wasn't no thang. His voice was chilling. The entire room didn't move once while he talked. My mother got on my nerves, but I couldn't imagine having to go through that.

Afterward a girl named Tiana, who was one of those loud types of chicks, gave him a big hug. They both started crying. The room exploded with cheers. I can't lie. I felt a little emotional, which was strange because it was for something that didn't have to do with Rashid. But then I started to think about my brother. And the room started to close in on me.

Two other kids shared how violence affected them. I started to tune out. That was the only way I was going to get through it. I was praying, well not really praying, more like wishing for the entire night to be done with. Eventually Dr. McKenzie went over how violence affects us all even if we don't realize it. She gave us advice for dealing with violence, but I didn't pay too much attention. Maybe I should have. After asking us if we had any questions, she said she had a treat for us.

Natasha.

"I keep telling you how talented our crew is," Dr. McKenzie said. "And if anyone wants to perform in the upcoming weeks, see me after tonight's session to sign up. Many of you know that I've been trying to get Tasha to dance for months now. She's ab-

solutely amazing, but as we all know, a perfection-
ist. She didn't want to grace our stage—" Robin
pointed to the broke down setup and the group
laughed "—until her piece was perfect. All I know is
that Ms. Thing can dance and I can't wait to see her
on Broadway one day. You will all be able to say I
knew here when! Please celebrate crew member,
Natasha Mayfield."

The room exploded with whoops, hollers and "go-
girls." Natasha's camel-colored face managed to turn
slightly red as she approached the stage. I hadn't
really paid too much attention to her earlier. During
the express yourself part of the session, I did
remember her talking about being excited about
some dance competition and trying to get her foster
mother to get along with her cousin.

From the moment that she made her first movement, a horizontal leg lift that demonstrated both
grace and strength, I was mesmerized. And I don't
think I've ever been mesmerized before. In a black
leotard and leggings, Natasha moved like she con-
trolled air. Her body rocked with the African rhythm
that blasted from Dr. McKenzie's old-school boom
box. At first, I couldn't interpret what I was
watching. Dancing to me was the two-step. For the
ladies, it was backing it up or dropping it. What
Natasha was doing was angel-like. An overwhelming feeling flushed over me. I wanted to touch her,

an impulse that I fought by gripping my hands together. Despite how hard I tried, though, I couldn't look away.

She danced for more than five minutes while the entire group watched in amazement. Her performance was like a tug-of-war between two parts of her—one who wanted to live fully and the other who wanted to drift. At the end of the routine, she ended holding herself like she accepted both parts.

I got the message. I understood. And I found myself standing up and clapping for her with the other crew members as she gathered herself from the floor and took a bow.

I wanted to tell her how much I liked the way she moved. I wanted to tell her how much she did her thing and that she was a real dancer, not like those chicks who shook what their mothers gave them in videos. But I said nothing. I just tried not to stare when she returned to her seat.

"We are a crew," Dr. McKenzie said at the end of the session. The group all agreed by doing this weird group-hug thing. She said she learned early on the importance of fostering positive group interaction. She saw too many young people lose their lives to gangs because they were looking for connection, family.

I was beginning to know loneliness like I knew my last name, the one that tied me to a dying family.

Rashid used to be my crew. I wanted a new one, but wasn't sure if I was ready for it.

When I left the church, I saw Natasha waiting for her ride. I wanted to go up to her, but I knew it would be dumb for me to stand in front of her without saying anything, just staring. So I headed to my mother's car instead.

Moms didn't bother to ask me how the first night went. She was probably tired of seeing my shoulders shrug. But she didn't notice the smile on my face either.

During the following week, I found myself dreaming about something other than the negative turn in my life. At school, the days sped by as I imagined Natasha on stage killing it—the pain, the bad emotions.

nineteen

MISS understand

On Thursday night, I left a note for my mother to remind her about Straighten It Out. I was determined to see Natasha again. It worked.

During the next meeting, Dr. McKenzie approached me during the break. I was packing my small paper plate with cookies.

"Well, Avery, what do you think so far?" She flashed her perfect smile. She must have had braces growing up.

I finished the rest of the chocolate chip cookie in my mouth, like I was going to say something. But instead I gave her one of my half shrugs and picked up a cup of red punch.

She whipped out a small notepad and blue pen.

"Write your response here," she said. I looked at her like she just tricked me into a confession.

Bothered, I put my cup down. I wrote, "It's cool" and handed her the pad.

"Good. You're not just writing that so that I'll leave you alone, are you?" she asked jokingly.

I did want her to leave me alone, but I was feeling Straighten It Out, or at least I was feeling Natasha. I wasn't sure if that was the same thing.

"You a Wizards fan?" she asked while grabbing a cookie.

I looked at her like she stole something, because she partly did. Basketball was a topic that was off limits. It didn't matter if she knew it or not. I tried to keep my cool. I knew how doctors like her worked—using trickery to get you to open up and talk. I wasn't falling for the okey-doke. I shook my head. Part of me was lost in the air between us.

"Really, I just figured you were a die-hard fan because of that Wizards jersey you're wearing." It was Rashid's and it was old, but I didn't care. I was annoyed, though. She was really trying to push me into a corner where I would have to face my emotions with nowhere to run. My only choice: breakdown. I didn't think I had the energy to fight her.

I rubbed my stomach and motioned to the door. "Oh, of course," she said when she realized that I was excusing myself to the bathroom. I walked out of the room and tried to catch my breath.

When I returned, break was over. Dr. McKenzie had the group pair off for what she called two-ways, where we talked with a partner about whatever was on our mind.

She put me with Natasha. "I want you two to connect today," she said. "I know that you're enjoying silence right now, Avery, but I think Natasha's okay with that."

Sweaty palms. Drips of it formed on my forehead. I started chewing on my nails all before Natasha opened her mouth. She looked even better than the first day I saw her. She had on this T-shirt that read, "Dance Machine." It was one of those tight tees that girls rocked and guys liked. Her jeans were tight. Not like suffocating tight, but they fit in the right places. You could tell she wasn't one of those girls who went all crazy over clothes, but that she still knew how to dress.

"I do understand silence," was the first thing out of her mouth. "That's why I prefer to talk through dance." My face smiled without my permission.

She did all the talking. Not because she had to. Not because she was selfish like Ricardo, but because she understood what I was going through. She didn't press me to utter any words for the sake of talking. Instead, for the remaining thirty minutes, she recounted comical and horrific stories from being in foster care. I hung on to her every word.

"She had a different wig for each day of the week," Natasha said as she let out a laugh that sounded like the beat for a song. She was talking about one of her super-weird foster mothers.

"On Monday, she was a fake Oprah, and on Tuesdays she was a low-budget Tyra Banks. She swore down that those cheap joints made her pretty. She looked like Shrek only with hair. And they stunk, too, smelled like wet trash." Natasha clapped her hands and stomped her feet at her jokes. I smiled. Hard.

Then she gave me the lowdown on Straighten It Out. "I've been coming here for about six months," she revealed. "At first, I was like this is wack, a waste of time. But my foster mother forced me and I really had no choice. So I started to listen to other people's stories and realized that I wasn't alone, you know?"

I shook my head like I knew.

"Then I started to share and that's when I really noticed a change."

Even without offering Natasha a "for real" or "that's crazy," she told me that I was one of the best listeners she ever met. I didn't need to talk to let her know that I cared what she said.

Through my silence, the two of us—one tortured and one recovering—got to know one another.

twenty

the detention center

DINNER at my house felt like detention, except for the fact that food was involved. Since Rashid's death, my mother's meals hadn't tasted much better than what the school cafeteria served. On Saturday night, we had bland corn and overcooked baked chicken that would probably bounce off the wall if anyone threw it.

Dinner used to be the time when we would all get together. Moms was serious about dinner; her boys, all three of them, couldn't miss it or that was their asses. But now we just sat at the table trying to avoid looking into each other's eyes. I stared at the yellow kernels of corn on my plate. Pops glared at the empty wall facing him. And my mother concentrated on nothing. Sometimes we took turns trying to act like one day we would return to being a happy unit.

Tonight was Pops'.

"I ran into Samuel and Theresa at the grocery store." No response from my mother. I knew the conversation wasn't going in a good direction.

My father continued. "They said that the city is doing a lot of changes in the surrounding areas around our neighborhood." He paused, leaving enough time for my mother to fuss. She sat and did nothing. "We should consider moving back to our house to save money, so we're not paying for two residences. Then down the line, purchase another property. We could rehab it and flip it for a profit."

If I didn't know any better, I would have thought that my father threw back a couple shots of Henny before dinner to prepare him for bringing up the old neighborhood. But my father didn't touch anything with alcohol after the death of his father from liver cancer.

"There's still no progress with Rashid's case," she said without acknowledging what my father had just said. "I can't believe no one has come forward yet. I've posted hundreds of fliers. I know someone knows something. A bunch of cowards. We're talking about a life here—the life of my child!" She threw her fork down and grabbed her forehead with both hands like she was trying to massage the headache that hadn't left since Rashid was buried.

I felt trapped under a fallen building and wanted desperately to be rescued. I wondered if blurting out Trevor's name would make my family normal again.

My father noticed the discomfort on my face. "Honey, I know you're upset," he said to my mother. "But maybe we can talk about something that doesn't have to deal with the case tonight? Hmm, what do you think?" He gently rubbed her left hand, the one with her wedding ring.

She pulled her arm away and threw her napkin onto her rubber chicken. She pushed herself out of her chair all dramatic like and stood up like she wanted to be counted. Tears bubbled slowly in her eyes. Sixty seconds passed. Then another minute. She shook her head and fired, "Y'all clean up."

My father and I ate the rest of our meal in silence and then loaded the dishwasher without saying a word.

twenty-one

dreams deferred

RICARDO and I were chilling at our usual table in the cafeteria. He was talking as usual and I was half listening, zoning out. I wasn't sure if Ricky was actually becoming cooler or if I liked the fact that being around someone who was as self-absorbed as him made me forget about my own life. Dude talked so much trash it was amazing that he wasn't sickened by the smell of it all. But I thought he was harmless.

October rolled through the county, bringing with it cooler temperatures, a distinct treelike smell and shades of orange, brown and maroon. I was settled into my new routine, far from happy, just settled. I spent the majority of my time looking forward to Fridays, or more accurately, to seeing Natasha.

During the week, my mother took and picked me up from school before heading off to her job to solve Rashid's case. I sat through my classes without making a sound. I had no friends, unless you counted Ricardo, and I wasn't sure yet if I could really call him one.

I made no effort to join any after-school activities as my father suggested. Normal teenage things— hanging out downtown, going to the park on Sundays to shoot the shit, hollering at girls—didn't appeal to me either.

I preferred drowning in the past where Rashid was there to save me.

"I knew you was going to be a boy before Mom and Dad did," Rashid told me once while we sat on the front steps. It was a ninety-degree day in Baltimore, which meant for houses without air, you chilled outside where it was usually a little cooler.

"Man, you're joking," I said. "You were only two years old."

"I was almost three," Rashid said in his defense. "But I'm telling you. Ask Mommy. I told her that a boy was in her stomach. I wanted a brother so bad. Maybe I didn't know all of what that meant, but I know I wanted a little me." Rashid finished the last of his egg custard snowball. Our block was hot. Not just from the weather, but from all the neighbors outside trying their best to cool off. If someone had pulled out a grill and some music, it could have been a block party.

"You didn't want a sister?"

"I mean, I would have been happy with a sister, but I think brothers have a special bond. We did everything together, almost like now. But we did even more stuff back in the day." Rashid wiped his face with the towel that rested on his shoulder.

"What if we weren't brothers?" I asked.

"What you mean?

"I mean what if Mom never had you or never had me? What if you were an only child?"

"I would hate it," Rashid said quickly.

"Yeah, it would suck." I wrapped my arm over my eyes to block the sun.

"I think it would be lonely. Like Jon-Jon. I think he acts like he does because he doesn't have a brother or a sister. So he always wants to be in the center of everything." I laughed at the thought of Jonathan, a kid we grew up with. We didn't like hanging out with him because he always whined about something.

"I got friends," Rashid continued. "But they can't compare to my lil' bro." Rashid grabbed the top of my head and shoved it. "You got brothers fighting like they enemies. That's crazy, you know?" I shook my head.

"I was there when you were born. You feel me?

The day that you came into this world, I was in the hospital. And I was mad excited to see you, like for real. It's crazy when you think about it. We came from the same mother and father." I thought about it. We were as close as two people could get.

"Yo, I was about to stomp him," Ricardo said while we waited at the lunch table for the bell to ring. It snapped me out of my reminiscing. "He's lucky Mr. Barnard came walking down the hallway." I just shook my head. Ricky excelled at frontin' and smack talking. I knew that Rashid would have pulled Ricky's card a long time ago, but I let Ricky have his fantasies as I held tight to my memories. I drifted through the rest of the school day with Rashid on my mind.

That night, like every night that I laid in bed, I imagined what happened that day on the court. I envisioned that Rashid's team was smashing their opponents because Rashid didn't lose. Don't get it twisted. Rashid wasn't one of those winners who losers wanted to punch in the mouth. He was like any other player with skills, but his shit talking was all in fun. He never crossed the line by insulting some dude's mother or telling them where they could go. I saw him trying to cool any heat between Trevor and Darryl into the small breeze. He probably told both parties that "it ain't that deep." He could have even gotten the two to give each other dap before going on with the game. When Trevor returned with the gun, Rashid might have seen it and told him to think about what he was about to do. He might of said, "It ain't worth it, main man." Even in his final moments, I was sure that Rashid was a shining light in the midst of darkness.

That night while I played the scene out in my head in the dark, quiet room while wearing tattered boxers and a dingy Gatorade T-shirt that Rashid and I copped for free at a summer festival in Druid Hill Park, my brother spoke to me.

Rashid's voice didn't sound like it normally did— that night it was a little high-pitched but forceful. Regardless of the differences in how it came out, I knew it was Rashid from the chills that zapped my body.

"You need to live," he told me. The words thundered around me. "Rashid?" I called out softly. There was no response, but that didn't matter. I had the answer I was looking for.

I smiled for the remaining three hours I had left in bed.

That morning while my parents were rushing around getting ready to start their days, I asked if there were any more Cheerios left. My mother burst out into sobs at the sound of my voice. With widened eyes, my father looked at me like he'd seen the second coming of his son. Then he ran to the store to buy more of my favorite cereal.

twenty-two

reintroduction

I didn't waste my words. And I didn't bother to tell my teachers that I was talking again. A few of them along with my classmates were freaked out when I answered a question in class. Others thought I was faking the entire time.

"Anyway, she tried to lie and say it was her first time," Ricky said while we were in the lunch line getting our food. He always talked loud enough so everyone in a five-foot radius could hear him. Ricky turned and smiled at the girl behind him who had sucked her teeth.

Lunch was really the only time that we talked during school. Ricky had told me he was supposed to be in the gifted and talented program with me, but managed to get kicked out of it so he could "keep it real" in the other classes. Apparently to Ricky, being smart meant you were a punk. I didn't bother arguing with his backward thinking.

"Why do you talk so much trash?" I finally asked. It was a question that burned at me since I met him.

Ricky took a step back and gave me a weird look. He had never heard my voice. "Yo, you sound like a chipmunk," he joked. "When did you start talking?"

Kids in line started looking at me like I was some sort of freak.

"Yo, I'm just messing with you. I'm glad you've come back to the world of talking. Man, we can get lots done now. I mean, it would be hard for us to two-team honeys with you being silent and all." He patted me on the back.

"So tell me about yourself, Avery. Why did you stop talking in the first place?" Ricky actually looked concerned as we moved along in the line.

So while we downed pizza and fries, I shared. I told him about Rashid. Ricky seemed to really care. I told him about Straighten It Out and about the angel I wanted to holler at. "That's what I'm talking about," Ricky said before telling me that he'd give me some tips to get at her. I even told Ricky about my parents and all their fighting. Ricky said he could relate. "My parents don't even talk to each other anymore," he told me. "I use it to my advantage, though."

For the first time in nearly two months, Ricky and I actually had a conversation. I realized that I had missed talking. Rashid was right. I had to start to living. I couldn't wait for Friday. It was on.

"I want you to partner with someone," Dr. McKenzie said after she read the announcements. "We're going to do a little role-playing activity. In a pair, I want you to pick an issue that young people deal with—peer pressure, drugs, sex, fighting with parents, gangs—whatever it may be. I want you to come up with a scene that illustrates the issue. Then you will act it out in front of the crew."

"Oh, Doc, I don't act," Walter complained as usual. He was one of those who griped about everything only to enjoy it in the end.

"I didn't say you did, Walter," she countered. "But try it, you may find an undiscovered talent." He shook his head in disagreement.

"Shoot, y'all gonna think I'm Will Smith in this piece," Oscar joked.

I hoped Natasha was going to pick me to do the scene. I glanced over at her quickly. She had a serious look on her face like she was thinking about something heavy. I hadn't spoken during the session yet. I wanted her to be the first one I talked to there.

"Okay, partner up. You'll have twenty minutes to come up with your scene and then you'll act them out on our lovely stage." Dr. McKenzie laughed at her joke.

I waited. Natasha was still lost in her own world. I didn't want her to get scooped up by anyone, although it seemed that the others were almost all paired up. *Man, stop being scared,* I told myself.

I walked over to her. "You got a partner?"

Natasha smiled like she meant it. Then, out of nowhere, she got up and gave me a hug. I was completely thrown off by the public display of affection, even though I knew that's what crew members did. I just didn't expect Natasha to do it to me. But I liked it. I liked it a lot. She smelled like vanilla and strawberries.

"I like your voice," she said after the embrace. "It's soothing."

"Thanks," was all I could think of. I was still bugging from the tightness of her hug. None of the lines that I had prepared to say came to mind. So I smiled with my teeth showing.

"Let's get started, partner." That easily, it was decided that we would work together.

"So what do you want to do?" she asked me.

"I don't know," I said honestly.

"Well, we could act like we're out on a date and you're trying to get some, but I'm not trying to hear it."

"Whoa." I felt my nerves tighten. For a minute, I

could visualize that scene, but I didn't want to look like a sucker.

"You sure you want to do that? Maybe we could do something dealing with school." I wanted a topic that was going to be safe. Acting out something dealing with sex? With Natasha?

"No, this is real. It happens all the time." She smoothed back her bun and put her pen in her mouth while she thought about the details.

It wasn't real for me. I wondered why she wanted to reject me. Was she trying to hint something? I was paranoid.

"Why wouldn't you give me any?" I was surprised by my own boldness.

She thought for a moment and said, "Because I don't know you like that. It could be like the second time we've hung out. That's too soon."

I was thinking about real life. Natasha was thinking about the skit.

"True." I felt a little better about her answer. "All right, so what do you want me to say?" I had never tried to get some from a female so I really didn't know how it worked. My thoughts about sex came from the dudes around the way, television, Rashid and Pops.

Natasha gave me a funny look. Her eyes squinted while she cocked her head. Then she smiled.

"Okay, we could be in your car and you could be dropping me off. First you say how much fun you had at the movies. And like, really act like you had a good time. Like going to the movies with me was the best day of your life. Then tell me how good I look in my outfit. Like, 'Girl, did I tell you how good you lookin' in those jeans? Damn, you making me wanna do something.' Then I'll giggle and be like, 'For real?' in a sweet, little voice."

She sounded like she had been through this situation a million times.

After she wrote down the first part of the script, she continued.

"Then ask if anyone is home. When I answer no, you ask to come in. I'll say that I'm not allowed to have company. Then you say—"

"How about we just end it there," I spoke up.

"That's not realistic."

"Why not? Not all guys are trying to get some," I said, trying to defend myself and the rest of the good dudes.

"Really? I haven't met any yet," she said.

"You've met me," I said with Rashid's swagger. I wondered if my brother was talking through me.

Natasha flashed me a quick smirk, then focused again on finishing the script. My game was shot down like an enemy plane.

"Okay, so after I tell you I'm not allowed to have company, then you can say something like, 'Well who's gonna know?'"

"Dudes really talk like that?" I started to think the dialogue sounded silly.

"What?" Natasha said without looking up from the white paper Dr. McKenzie provided us with to record our scenes.

"Nothing, it just sounds corny," I said in a way to make sure I didn't offend her.

"Well, how would you say it?" Natasha fired back.

"I mean, it just sounds like game. I guess I would be a little more, you know, genuine."

"More genuine about tryin' to get some?" Natasha asked with a slight laugh.

"Naw, just more genuine period. I mean the way you wrote it, it's like the dude is putting on an act."

"Exactly." Natasha pointed her index finger in my direction.

I thought about it—about how some of the cats around the way used to speak and how Rashid would always call their bluff.

"Yo, I ain't into playing girls," Rashid would say. "'Cause that mess will come back to haunt you. If you like her, you like her. If you don't like her but she like you, you got to let her know how you really feel. You can't be a jerk and take advantage of the situation. That mess will come back and bite you in the ass. That's why all these cats running around with babies by chicks they can't stand."

I was nervous about performing with Natasha.

For one, I wasn't the type who liked to be in front of crowds, period. Secondly, it was with Natasha. How was I supposed to pretend to want to get with her when I actually wanted to get with her? Maybe not in her jeans, but I definitely wanted us to be close.

Keisha and Tracey went first. They were both mad quiet, but they were like different people when they got on stage. They performed a skit about being overweight. Keisha is heavy and Tracey look like she need to eat more. Tracey played the mean girl and Keisha showed how people should stick up for themselves and be confident no matter what.

When Dr. McKenzie called us, the crew got hyped. Most of them had seen me talking to Natasha and they were giving me props for getting over my silence. It's crazy because I was going from no talking to acting in front of a group. Your boy was nervous. But Natasha grabbed my hand and led me to the broke-down stage. Her skin felt silky like one of those night-gowns at Victoria's Secret. The jumping in my stomach got more intense.

I read her lines just as she wrote them. I tried to put some emotion into it like I saw Denzel or Will do, but acting wasn't my thing. Natasha was real into, though. She played the whole naive-girl role real well. The group gave us another huge round of applause when we were done.

"What did we think about Natasha and Avery's scene?" Dr. McKenzie asked.

"I thought it was real," Ramona said. "Dudes are always trying to get you to have sex with them, even if you don't know them that well."

"That's not true," I said out of nowhere. I was thinking it, but didn't mean to say it aloud.

"Go on," Dr. McKenzie encouraged.

"I'm just saying, not all guys want to, uh, you know, get with girls in that way. Some of us want to just talk." I could hear snickers from the audience and for a minute I felt like a real punk for saying something like that.

"He's right," Hector said.

"Yeah," Dejuan added. "It's like society puts pressure on us to make us feel like we always gotta be chasing girls, like we ain't a man if we ain't hittin' it."

"My brother always says, uh, said, that having sex can be good, but it can also be bad and that you got to be smart about it." That was the first time I brought up Rashid in front of the crew. The moment the words flipped out of my mouth, I wanted to take them back.

"Just because I'm a dude don't mean I want to be sexing all the time," Hector agreed.

"What do others think?" Dr. McKenzie asked the girls.

"I wish more guys felt that way," Natasha answered. "I mean, maybe they do, but they just front like they don't." She looked at me while she spoke. We caught eyes for a few seconds, but then I had to look away. That was definitely a punk move.

We talked for the rest of the meeting about guys, girls, sex and pressure. It was a really good conversation. I was happy to be talking again.

That night and every night I listened to hear Rashid's voice. It was reason enough to look forward to living.

twenty–three

spoiled rotten

It was the second blunt Ricardo had rolled and smoked by himself. We were chilling in his apartment-sized bedroom. The joint had its own bathroom and Jacuzzi tub. Ricardo had his own level in the house. His peoples slept upstairs and hardly came down to his "kingdom" for fear of invading his personal space. Ricardo ran the household like he paid bills.

And what a household it was. His peoples were paid like some Beverly Hills cats. Their house was in the cut, by itself. You had to drive up this long-ass driveway to reach it. His house could have been on MTV *Cribs* and outshined tons of rappers' homes. There were all these fancy paintings and expensive-looking furniture that you didn't want to sit on. All around the house were pictures of Ricky and his parents—them happily smiling on beaches, at events where Ricky sported a tuxedo and in the snow in ski outfits. And his spot was clean. Like eat-off-the-floor clean. Ricky told me that a maid came every week to make sure it stayed that way.

I've only met his peoples twice. It seemed like they were never home. His father was some big-shot lawyer and his mother didn't work, but she was busy like she had a job. They never ate dinner together like my family used to.

"I can't believe you've never smoked before," Ricardo said with a blunt hanging out of the side of his mouth. "I think you be fakin'. You ain't from the city."

"You act like every cat from the city gets high or something," I shot back.

He and I had been hanging out at his house for a few hours. I liked being over there because I didn't have to do nothin'. Plus there wasn't any fighting. I felt like I could breathe even with all the marijuana smoke.

"Check this out," Ricardo said in his cocky voice.

He opened the bottom drawer of his black leather dresser. It was stacked to the top with weed.

"I'm in business, man!" Ricardo shouted like he lived alone. He grabbed handfuls of the green and threw it in the air. He watched them scatter onto his plush tan carpet.

"Where did you cop it from?" I was curious.

"You know my man Boo." Ricardo name-dropped. I knew Ricardo talked too much from the moment we met. I was more or less testing Ricky's gangster even though I didn't think he had much.

"Where did you get the money to buy all this weed?" I asked in disbelief. Then I thought about how long it took Rashid and I to save the two G's that was in our savings stash. Months.

"From my peoples," Ricky said. He looked like he wanted to pat himself on the back. He put out the half-smoked blunt in his Bob Marley ashtray and threw the remainder over the dead legend's face.

"Your parents gave you money to buy drugs?"

"Naw, they ain't that cool. I told them I needed it for a trip that the Du Bois boys are taking." Ricky was in tons of groups for rich kids. But he hardly went to the meetings. I remember Ricky telling me that his parents didn't want him missing any important social functions involving their kind of people. Only time his parents really got angry was when he missed one of his lessons. That got them in a "huff," Ricardo had said.

"Yeah, so you just gonna sell dimes and nicks?" I wondered.

"Well, I'm gonna see how fast I can get this off my

hands." Ricardo rubbed his palms together like he was developing some evil plan. I looked back at the drawer. It could fit a small child.

"But honestly, selling small baggies ain't really my style. After this is gone, I'm gonna look into something heavier. I know that Boo got alternatives." I knew what Ricky meant by alternatives. Earlier that day he told me he was going to stop going by Pretty Ricky. Instead he wanted people to start calling him Freeway Ricky, after the notorious drug dealer who had spent mad years in prison. But Ricardo didn't care about that part.

"What do you need the money for? Don't your peoples hook you up?" I pointed around the spacious room for emphasis. In one corner, he had one of those basketball shooting games that you see at arcades. A flat screen that graced another wall was on mute, but featured a bikinied brown girl who was seductively eyeing the camera. Ricky's closet was the size of my old room. Shelves stacked to the ceiling were filled with neatly folded designer T-shirts. His prized tennis shoe collection was kept untouched in their original boxes.

"Well, if I follow the laws of the street—I got the money. Now I need the power and respect." Ricardo pointed to the green clumps of weed that sprinkled the carpet.

"You sound ridiculous," I finally admitted.

"Whatever. You know I'm right," Ricardo said as he grabbed a Corona from his mini refrigerator. "Want one?" he offered.

I waved a "no." I've drunk a couple of beers before with Rashid at Tavon's, but I never really got into the taste.

"Look at her booty bounce," Ricardo pointed to his forty-two-inch screen. "This is why I had to get the big boy. Can you imagine trying to look at that ass on a nineteen-inch?" He laughed as he reclined in his leather chair like a man who just pulled a twelve-hour work shift.

"Yo, you talk about women like you hate them or something," I responded.

"I don't hate women," Ricardo said with a serious face. "I just love them from behind," he hunched over and belted out a mean laugh.

I was learning a lot about Ricky that day. He told me how he ended up at Macon. He had started a small fire in the boys' bathroom at his former private school; a last straw for the administration who requested his immediate removal. His parents finally caved in and sent him to public school more so to avoid additional embarrassment from their circle of friends.

Rosa, the cook and Ricardo's former nanny—he made it clear that she didn't look after him anymore because he's too damn old for a babysitter—acted as the go-between for him and his parents. She changed Ricardo's first diaper when his mother said she was too tired to wipe her son's behind. Rosa was a plump woman, who resembled a brown M&M. If it wasn't for her motherly feelings toward Ricardo, she'd be back in her native Puerto Rico with her extended family. At least that's how Ricky told it.

Between his father's board meetings and his mother's social outings to museums, charity events and weekly beauty schedule, his peoples didn't have much time for family stuff—except the annual trip they took together. They made sure to take plenty of pictures so that they could plaster them around the house to make it seem like they were one happy family.

A knock at the door made me jump. Weed was still scattered on the floor. Two empty Corona bottles that Ricardo downed in less than twenty minutes were front and center on the dresser. Ricardo was cool, though. I was shook.

"Damn, what you all nervous about?" Ricardo said jokingly as he bopped to the door. He opened it just enough to see one of Rosa's eyes.

"Yes, *abuela?*" he asked while positioning his body so she couldn't see anything on the other side of the door.

"I can smell that nasty drug all the way downstairs," she said with her heavy accent.

"*Abuela,* you're getting old," Ricardo said, sounding like one of those rich, spoiled kids on television. "Ain't no drugs up in here. Right, Avery?" Ricardo announced. He looked over at me but kept the door half-closed.

I didn't answer but instead shot him a dirty look. I didn't want any part of the drugs. That included lying about them, especially to an old lady like Rosa.

"I'm going to have a talk with your parents tonight," she said with her stubby finger in his face. I think they both knew that didn't mean much.

"Do whatever makes you happy," he said before slamming the door in the face of the woman who raised him.

twenty-four

closer

"DO you ever feel like you are going to explode?"
Natasha asked me as we waited for our rides
together. We were the only two left from that night's
session. Dr. McKenzie waited inside doing some paperwork. It was unusual for my mother to be late,
but she had already called to tell me she was on the
way. It would be a few minutes, though, because she
was traveling from our old neighborhood. I told her
to take her time. I enjoyed every moment I had with
Natasha when it was just us.

"Every day," I responded naturally. It started
getting dark earlier. By the time we were finished
with our session, the sun that was chilling earlier in
the day had completely disappeared. The stars took

its place and provided a sexy light for our conversation. Girls would call it romantic.

Natasha thought long about my response like she was thinking of an answer for a test. Using her fingers, she combed through her hair, which almost reached her shoulders. It didn't matter how she rocked her hair—in a ponytail, straight back or curly—she always looked good, real good. I hated when chicks wore fake hair. But it wasn't just her hair that made me all hot inside. It was her.

"I thought I was the only one," she said after a few minutes. We were sitting on the church steps. Our knees were touching.

"I remember telling this guy I liked that, you know, sometimes I feel like I'm going to explode and he said I was crazy. Do you think I'm crazy, Avery?"

I thought about it for a moment. Not the crazy part, but about her liking someone. I wondered what the dude was like and if I was anything like him.

"If you're crazy, I'm crazy," I replied. She smiled like it was her first time.

"What do you think being in love feels like?" Natasha asked without looking me in the face. I'm glad she didn't because I was probably blushing a little. I never thought too much about love like that. Never really had a chance.

Before I could think of a good answer, she continued. "I mean, you hear people talk about it like it's the greatest thing ever. Then some people make it seem like it's the worst thing to happen to you. My aunt used to tell me to never fall in love."

Natasha rarely spoke about her family. And when she did, I felt funny asking questions even though I wanted to know more. I didn't want her to feel like I was trying to be in her business too much. I figured if she wanted me to know, she'd say so.

"I wonder if it feels like I feel when I'm dancing. Like dancing is hard. Sometimes I leave the studio so tired, you know?" I nodded my head. "But it makes me feel so good at the same time. Maybe that's how love is."

It made sense to me.

"Man, I remember at first, I didn't even want to dance," she said laughing. "Ms. Jameson forced me. She pretty much dropped my ass off at the studio and left me there. She had read in one of those female magazines that children involved in stuff outside of school were less likely to get in trouble. She didn't want me running the streets like I used to. She figured I needed a place to burn up all that energy."

Gwendolyn Saurent's, the dance studio that Tasha goes to, is pretty well-known in Baltimore. Even I had heard of it because I had seen the dancers at the Afram festival one summer. They were always doing shows around the city. Natasha said the owner, Gwendolyn, was a straight-up character. She opened the studio in the early seventies when folks weren't really checking for a black woman to run her own business. But she kept at it, fighting off the haters and the studio went on to become real popular and not just in Baltimore. Tasha says many of the dancers travel around the world performing.

"Gwendolyn strolls in with her poodle, carrying him like he's a baby. She's always rocking Chanel shades and she'll be like, 'No, darling, your technique is all wrong,' or 'Oh, darling, you remind me of myself.' She's a trip."

"So what happened when you went up there the first time?"

"The first day was real eye-opening. I had never seen males do anything else besides the two-step. Usually dudes just post up on the wall at a party and wait for a chick to rub all up on their stuff. But these dudes, they were moving like spirits or something. Lifting girls in the air like they were weightless. I couldn't stop watching them." I thought back to the first time I saw Natasha dance. I felt the same way.

"I mean, I shake my thang at a party, grindin', droppin' it," she continued. "But I knew nothing about dance, real dance. I guess I fell in love that day. Not with the guys, but with the movement, the way they used their bodies. The control they had over their bodies. It was beautiful. I wanted that type of control and I wanted to be beautiful."

I wanted to tell her she was beautiful, but the words wouldn't form.

"But I was still so nervous. The girls were rocking these tiny leotards and spandex stuck to their body. I didn't think there was any way I was fitting into one of them. I wasn't into showing my body. I had on a purple sweat suit and some dogged Reeboks. I told Ms. Jameson that if I had to dance in one of those outfits, it was never happening. She told me that I had to stop being so negative and give things a chance. So I did. And I liked it. And I was good. So good that the school created a scholarship program just so girls and boys like me could learn to dance. They saw something in me. And I wasn't gonna let them down."

That was two years ago.

Natasha said Ms. Jameson was determined to build her back up emotionally (Straighten It Out), physically (dance) and spiritually (church every Sunday, through rain, sleet or snow).

"So do you think it's working?" I asked.

"What?"

"Your foster mother's plan to build you back up."

"I'm a totally different person," she said. I was happy for her that she changed for the better, but part of me wanted to know the old Natasha, too.

Her ride arrived in an older body Lexus. Our time was cut short. I expected to see her foster mother, but instead it was some dude. She said it was her cousin. Slim was all up in my face like he knew me. She gathered her book bag and hurried toward the car. Then she waved back at me. Even her wave was sexy.

twenty-five

Below Average

I only really felt alive when I was around Natasha or when I was in bed listening for Rashid. In the rest of life, I wasn't doing much more than the minimum—breathing, eating, bathing, going to the bathroom and hanging with Ricky.

My teachers started hounding me for my lack of participation in class. They said they expected more from me. Mr. King, my world history teacher, told me he wondered how I got into the gifted and talented program in the first place. I had turned in the last two tests with only my name filled in. In gym, I sat on the bleachers in a dreamy haze, reminiscing of times when me and Rashid played kickball on the streets of our old neighborhood.

My classmates were pretty much over making fun of me. The taunts began as "he a punk" for not standing up for myself, to "yo is weird" when they realized I didn't talk, to "he is crazy, I ain't messin' with him."

Then one morning during homeroom, I was called to the principal's office. Mrs. Thompson was one of those old-school administrators. She didn't mess around. Her students' business—their grades, their lives, their bad behaviors—was her business.

"Mr. Washington," she began while she pulled her glasses off her eyes and let them hang on to her chest. "I'm very glad to have you here at Macon. I know from your past record at Central that you're an exceptional student. So that's why I'm concerned about your midterm grades. You don't have above a C in any of your classes. In three classes, you are currently carrying a D-average."

In the past, going to the principal's office meant I was getting some sort of award. I'd never thought I would be called because I was in danger of getting kicked out of the gifted and talented program. I also never thought that I wouldn't really care. Grades used to really matter to me. Now they were just letters on a page.

"Now your mother shared with me the recent tragedy that your family is working through. My heart goes out to you. But I know you're capable of doing better and it's my job to ensure that you succeed. What will it take for you to get your grades up?"

I wanted to say that having my brother back would do it, but I knew she couldn't make that happen.

"I don't know."

She gave me a disappointed look like my grandmother used to give me and Rashid anytime we weren't acting perfect. I hated letting down old people.

"Well, I am going to call your parents tonight and together we're going to develop a plan to get you back on track. Expect to see me again very soon." And then she sent me back to class.

"That don't count," Ricky said as he fixed the collar on his purple button-down shirt. That boy loved to rock female colors. We were at the lunch table finishing our hamburgers.

"What you mean it don't count? I was almost all the way in," I said defensively.

"Yeah, but you wasn't all the way in, so you didn't finish," Ricardo continued. "That means it don't count. The only good thing, bro, is you don't have to worry about her poppin' up pregnant and saying you the daddy," Ricardo snickered as he pulled out his brush to smooth down his waves. You never caught that fool without a brush. He told me that during the summer after ninth grade, he got contacts, ditched his bottle-cap glasses, shot up five inches and lost the baby fat he was carrying. Chicks started calling him Pretty Ricky and he ate it up. Back in my old neighborhood, pretty boys were never in.

"I wish one of these chicks I'm handlin' would try to pull some baby daddy stuff on me. I'm ghost." Ricardo made a mad dash with his hands.

"Whateva. Your parents would kill you, especially your moms." I countered. His mother would probably die of embarrassment if she found out that her perfect little son had gotten some girl pregnant. Mrs. Freedman was one of those uppity ladies who thinks her crap doesn't stink. She makes Ricardo take French lessons and horseback riding at some farm in Pennsylvania. I've never seen a real horse, let alone ridden one. "Cultured." That's what she told Ricky she was trying to make him.

"They wouldn't know. I wouldn't let it go that far. There's a clinic right on Washington Street next to the Popeyes. I wouldn't give the chick no dough, but I would give her bus fare." Ricardo burst out laughing and grabbed his stomach like he just said the funniest shit.

"That's messed up," was all I said. "But Tina said she liked it," I added although I was lying.

See this is what happened. Tina and I lived on the same block in my old neighborhood. She was batting

a C average in the body, looks and brain department, but she was mad cool. She smoked, so she
always smelled like funky cigarettes. When we were
in the second grade, she got in trouble for cussing at
the teacher. Her pops came to school with a belt and
beat her ass in the teachers' bathroom. She never
lived that down. To this day kids around the way
would joke her about it.

One day after school when Rashid was at drum
practice, she texted me and said I should stop by her
house. She went to private school, so I hadn't seen
her in a minute. I didn't think anything of it. I
stopped by her spot, her peoples weren't home. She
asked me to come to her room so she could show me
her cheerleading outfit. I still didn't think she wanted
to get at me because for as long as we had been
neighbors, she never really showed any interest in me.
We used to joke each other. She would call me big
head and I would call her a giraffe because she was
two feet taller than me. Other than that, we weren't
real close, but we'd always speak when we saw each
other on the streets.

Next thing I know we were in her pink room. It
felt like we were in a garden with all the flowery crap
she had all over the place. She started to kiss on my
neck. And it felt good, real good. No girl had ever
done that before. She was doing that and rubbing on
my chest. Then she kissed me in the mouth, but I

wasn't about to suck that cigarette crap off her tongue. So we stopped. She took my shirt off, then my pants. She asked me if I had protection. Of course I didn't because I had no idea she was trying to get down like that. And I wasn't completely sure if I wanted to get down with her like that anyway. My pops had given me and Rashid some condoms if we were ever in the situation when we needed them. He said he didn't want us having sex, but if we decided to do it, he wanted to make sure we didn't become fathers or catch a disease.

Tina knelt down on her faded pink carpet, grabbed an old Mickey Mouse lunchbox from under her bed. She released the metal latch and revealed a container full of condoms. She told me to pick one like they were pieces of candy. I chose a yellow one. She left me alone while I struggled to get the banana-colored rubber over my man. My hands were a little shaky. I mean, I wasn't nervous, just caught off guard. It was all happening so fast. I didn't really think about what was going on. I was just doing. Doing what Tina said. I finally slid the joint over my joint and she immediately jumped on me like some type of animal. Her green cotton panties were on the floor. She didn't have a bra on because she really didn't have anything to fill it. She pushed me down on her leafy comforter and started grinding like we were at a party and a slow jam was playing. Then she grabbed my joint and tried to direct it into her. All I saw was lots of hair so I'm not sure where she was putting my thing. It wasn't going in. Part of me wanted to ask her if it was her first time. But she might have asked me the same question and I didn't want to go there. She was getting all frustrated, so she got off of me and laid on her back. She spread her ashy legs and pulled me on top of her.

I tried to put it in, but it still wouldn't go. I didn't want to hurt her. I was trying to be gentle. She told me to hurry up because her mother was going to be home in a few minutes. Part of it got in, like the tip, but that was it. It felt good, though, but I started to get nervous that her moms might pop in at any moment, so I stopped.

Ricardo said he couldn't believe that I didn't continue. He said it wouldn't have taken me long to finish my business.

"But after we did it, she said she liked it," I said again to him. I had no idea why I was lying. I think Ricardo was rubbing off on me. Tina and I never spoke about it again.

"That's 'cause she was a virgin and didn't know any better," he said as he laid his necklace's diamond-encrusted cross medallion perfectly on his chest. "Pass along her number and I'll show her what it's really supposed to feel like."

"Whateva, man. You've only been hooking up for

girls for a few months. Now all of sudden you an expert?"

"You damn right I am," Ricky said while patting his chest. "You don't know how long I've been doing my thing. Shoot, I've been knockin' down chicks since I was a toddler." Ricardo laughed his same loud, unnecessary laugh. I shook my head and laughed, too.

"That's why you got to come to the next party that my man throws. You ain't a man yet, you like twenty-five percent of man. Mad chicks gonna be at this party. All of them down to make up for that seventy-five percent you missing." His eyes were lit up like traffic signals.

"I ain't tryin' to go to some corny County party," I said, although something about it sounded good. I hadn't been to a party or anything resembling one in a real long time. I felt like getting out.

"It ain't even in the County," Ricky replied.

"Where is it?" I asked.

Lunch was dismissed and we headed into the hallway. The halls of Macon resembled one of those multiracial Gap commercials. The school had black, brown, white, yellow and everything in between. But just because we went to school together didn't mean we hung together. Black stuck with black. White stuck with white. So much for Dr. King's dream. It was more like a fantasy.

"Somewhere near your old stomping grounds, on the Eastside."

"Where on the Eastside? Eastside ain't just one neighborhood and I don't hang out in hoods I'm not too familiar with." That was a rule that most city cats abided by.

"Man, first you scared to get some and then you scared to go to a party. I'm tryin' to tell you, it's gonna be off the chain. Why does it matter where it's at?"

"How off the chain?" I asked curiously.

"Yo, at the last one, drunk honeys were all over the place ready for a cat like me to give it to them." Ricardo talked without taking any breaths. "I knocked down this one chick and now she calls a brother like every day. I had to block her number, but she just calls me from other phones, throwing me off. But I can't really blame her. I mean, I did perform like a champ." He made a gesture with his hands that looked like he was shooting a basketball.

I had yet to see Ricky bag the amount of females he claimed he did. He kicked it with Taneisha, an average-looking girl with enormous breasts who claimed that she was half Indian. But it wasn't long before Taneisha moved on to one of the basketball players and Ricardo tried to front like he didn't care.

"The drinks were flowing. The buddha was right

and the chicks were ready. I was in ghetto heaven."
Ricky continued boasting.

"Who throws them?"

"My connect, Boo. And you got to know someone
to be up in there."

"Mrs. Thompson called today," my mother said
when I got into the car after school. I thought she
would give me a little time before she dug into me.

"Avery, you are a straight-A student. Your grades
are your ticket to college. Your father and I can't
afford to send you to college. I know you're going
through a lot, but you still have to do your part."

I looked out the window at all the students heading
home. Some had big smiles on their faces like their
days were just beginning. I was jealous of them.

I wondered what her part was—she spent all her
free time with her nose in files or sitting around the
police station but never coming home with answers.

"Have the police made any progress in Rashid's
case?" I knew I was going to a place that I probably
shouldn't have gone. I knew the police had no leads.
So did my moms. It showed all over her face.

"We're talking about you," she said. In one swoop,
she shut me down.

"I'm just not feeling school right now," I
answered honestly.

"Well, when do you think you'll start feeling it

again?" my mother asked. I wondered if she was giving me a choice. And I wished I could give her a date and time, but I had no idea.

I gave her a shoulder shrug.

"Well, that's unacceptable. You better come up with a plan to get back on track. Quickly."

She hurled the threat at me, but I didn't catch it.

twenty-six

twenty-one questions

"she keeps a notebook," I told Natasha the first time she came over to my house. We were in the living room. My mother was at the police station but said it was all right for Tasha to come over. She had met Ms. Jameson and thought Tasha was a "nice girl." Plus she preferred me home than to be over at friend's house. And she liked the fact that Tasha was a girl. She wasn't quite sure yet if young black men could be trusted around her remaining son, as if hanging out with black dudes or being seen with them might get me shot. My father agreed with her although he tried to act like he didn't.

Natasha flipped through the pages—all stuff about Rashid, which my mother kept in those plastic sleeves. There were articles about his shooting. Copies of fliers she created and posted around the neighborhood looking for my brother's killer, elementary school report cards and cheesy class pictures.

I didn't like looking at it because it was like stuffing Rashid into a three-subject notebook. His spirit was bigger than a neat collection of papers.

I was mixing some purple Kool-Aid when Natasha asked, "How did you feel when you found out?"

"Found out what?" I asked as I stirred the wooden spoon in the pitcher. She was standing real close to me. Too close. I knew what she was talking about, but I didn't feel like getting into my feelings. Chicks always wanted to know how you felt about something. I'm sure she wanted to know that I cried all my tears away. But I learned a long time ago that talking about Rashid too much always became tiring. My emotions collided and I ended up with a headache.

"I don't know," was all I said.

"You ever wonder why God gave humans the power to take away lives?" she asked and waited for a response. But I didn't think she wanted me to answer. I think she just wanted me to think about it.

She continued. "I mean shouldn't he be the only

one able to do that? Why should a knucklehead with a gun be able to determine your brother's fate? Why should a kid have so much power?"

Natasha threw me off sometimes when she asked those deep-ass questions. I never had answers for them, but sometimes I wished I did. I wanted to be able to answer why Natasha landed in foster care. Or why my brother was dead. Or why his killer was still running free. But I didn't have the answers. I just had more questions. No girl I knew talked like her. No girl I knew thought like she did. I wanted to be on her level.

Her face looked real intense. And I liked it that way, too. The lines in her forehead would appear and make her look older.

"Have you ever been in love?" Natasha asked next. We moved to the living room and were sitting on the couch with a small space between us. Natasha loved to talk about love. I felt like she had asked me that before. Like we already had that conversation, but I didn't mind having it again.

"Hell naw," I responded. I felt too young to be in love, although my parents met in high school, fell in love and got married. But it's different now. Marriage ain't really cool. And nobody seems to talk about love like it's important either.

"Me neither," she said. "I want to one day. I mean I want to be swept off my feet like I'm Cinderella or somebody. Am I tripping?" She looked up at me for an answer.

"Naw, you deserve a prince," I said. "Shoot, if I had a horse, I'd rescue you," I said jokingly.

She smiled a smile that I would pay for it.

It was corny but true. Natasha had been through hell with gasoline panties on, but she kept her head up like 2Pac once rapped.

"Dudes used to tell me they loved me just so they could hit it," she admitted. "Then they would throw me away like I was a piece of trash."

I didn't know what to say, so I didn't say anything. I just listened.

"I used to be real messed up. When I was thirteen this dude, he was like twice my age, told me that he really cared for me. I thought I loved him. How crazy is that?" She stopped and looked at me for a response.

"You didn't know better," I said.

"And after he got what he wanted, he wouldn't return my phone calls. I was searching for love because I hadn't gotten it from my parents."

Tasha had never really talked about her peoples. I wasn't sure if they were dead or in trouble or what.

"It was hard for my mother to love me because she hardly loved herself. She was seventeen when she had me. After she left the hospital she went to my father's house." Tasha paused.

"I mean, I don't know if I can even call him that. All he did was get my mother knocked up, he didn't help her. He just..." She took a deep breath like she had to prepare herself for what was coming.

"My aunt told me that my mother knocked on his door and left me on the doorstep. Apparently, she saw that in some movie and the baby lived a happy life. Can you believe that?"

I couldn't believe it. And I didn't know what to say to her. What do you say to something like that? But Tasha didn't really want an answer. She just wanted to know that I was there with her, following her, feeling her, understanding her.

"My aunt told me that my mother wanted me to have a good life. A few days after dropping me off, my mother killed herself at my aunt's house where she was living. My aunt found her dead on the floor in the bathroom. No note. No nothing. Gone just like that." I was hoping that Tasha didn't start crying because there would be no way for me to stop myself from doing the same. Her eyes weren't watering. But they were dark and slightly closed.

I always wondered how bad stuff had to be for someone to want to go away forever. As bad as I felt about losing Rashid, I never wanted to go away forever. Maybe for a little while until stuff got easier, but not forever.

"Her body died that day," she said. "But her spirit

had died years before that. She never had a chance."
I felt like Rashid was the opposite. His spirit was still
living, but his body was gone.

"Do you ever feel like your mother is talking to
you?" I asked. I hadn't told Tasha about Rashid
talking to me because I didn't want her to think I was
nuts.

"Not actually speaking. But sometimes I feel her.
You know?" She looked directly into my eyes and bit
down her on lower lip. She looked sexy and scared
at the same time.

"I know. I can feel Rashid." I put a smile on her
face. We understood each other and it felt good. She
moved closer to me on the sofa and grabbed my hand.
She just held it. Not tightly. Then she told me the rest
of her story.

"My father was twenty-seven years old when he
met my mother at a bus stop. Right there at the
corner of Pat Street and North Avenue. My aunt said
my mother probably had on something short and
tight because she felt that was the only way someone
would pay attention to her. My father could tell she
was damaged goods just by how she looked. He
hollered at her and they started getting close real
fast. Before no time, my mother popped up pregnant.
He already had a few kids and told her he didn't want
any more. This was the third time my mother had
been pregnant. She went to some clinic that she had

went to before, but for some reason this time she couldn't get the procedure for free. She didn't have any money, so she stayed pregnant. Sometimes I wonder, if she would have had money, there would be no me." That was a deep-ass thought. I had known Tasha for only a little while, but at that point I really couldn't have imagined how my life would have been if I hadn't met her.

"My father didn't want any more kids. He wasn't even really taking care of the ones he had. His mother was and so she made him go to Child Services. That's when the state became my parents."

"What about your aunt? Could you have lived with her?"

"I did for a little while until she was killed in a car accident."

Life is crazy. Because when you think you got it bad, you hear someone else's story and realize that everyone got stuff going on and sometimes much worse than you.

"It seems like you're doing well with Ms. Jameson," I said, trying to lighten the mood a little.

"Yeah, she's like my savior. I mean she ain't no joke. You know, I don't mess with Ms. Jameson, but I needed that tough love, you know?" She let go of my hand and smoothed her jeans. I tried to play it cool like I didn't care. My hand was still warm.

"For a long time, I was messed up in the head. I felt like no one loved me. In the beginning, I bounced from home to home in foster care. And I would fall for guys—foster brothers, dudes I met out—it didn't matter. They would fill me with lies about liking or loving me and I would feed off of it. Ms. Jameson, Straighten It Out and dance all showed me that I was worth more than I ever thought and that I deserved more."

"I wish things had worked out differently for both of us."

"I know what you mean," she replied. "Sometimes I wish I could go back and change things, you know? Like undo some of the mistakes I've made. Ms. Jameson says that as long as I learn from my mistakes, that's all that matters. But I don't know. Even as I change and become smarter, some people still think I'm the old me."

"I wish I could go back to the old me," I said. "That means Rashid would be here. I'm not sure how much the new me is really me."

She hugged me after I said that. And I felt a burst of life go through my body. We stayed like that for a few moments and I didn't want to let go.

"I should leave now," she said, looking at her watch. "Can't be late with Ms. Jameson." I walked her to the door.

"I really, uh, like talking to you," I said all awkward.

"Me, too," she said and gave me a kiss on my cheek. I felt like the man.

twenty-seven

i've got a story to tell

I was only going to do it because I had promised Doc. Telling a group of people—even the crew—my business was not really my style. When I was younger, I always dreaded when teachers forced me to get in front of the class and tell something about myself. I hated having tons of eyes staring at me waiting for me to say or do something stupid. If it wasn't for my pops, I would have had to say something at Rashid's funeral. My mother thought I should have, but my father disagreed and fought with her over it. I threatened to not attend the funeral, but we all knew that would have never happened. My father convinced my mother that it wasn't the right time or occasion to make me do something that made me feel uncomfortable.

Dr. McKenzie had been nagging me for a few weeks to tell the crew what happened. She said that sharing my story would not only help me, it would also make some of the other members feel better about losing someone they loved. Therapeutic was what she called it. One of her favorite words.

"Avery, we're ready to hear from you," she said after saying the announcements. My hands were sweaty. They felt like I had just washed them and didn't bother to dry them.

"Take your time," Natasha said to me before I went up. She told me to concentrate on her if I got nervous. I had to stand in the front and face the crew. Their chairs were laid out in a half circle.

When I got up there, I stared at Dr. McKenzie first. She was standing to the side. She gave me a gesture motioning for me to begin when I was ready. Then I looked at Natasha. She looked nervous for me. She began clapping and the entire group joined in. That comforted me a little. I could tell they were interested in what I had to say.

After a few minutes of dead silence, I gathered the courage to begin.

"You can probably look at me and tell that I'm not too special," I began. I was unsure where the words were coming from, but I let them fall out of my mouth and into their ears.

"But my brother, Ra—" it was hard for me to say his name. I liked to say it only around family and friends. I held on to for a little while before completing it. Then I let go.

"My brother Rashid was special. He was so special that he, he, uh, made me feel, you know, special." The group let out this sound like a sigh. They wanted me to continue.

I was staring at the ground by this point. I tapped my foot to help me get the rest of my story out.

"He was uh," I looked up at Dr. McKenzie. She gave me a head motion that told me to keep talking.

"He was uh, more than my brother. He was my best friend, too. I, I, uh, loved him more than I loved myself." The moment I said that, I realized that had been the truth. I never admitted it until then. I became scared about what I was going to say next. I felt exposed, like I was being too honest. But the crew seemed to hang on my every word. Maybe I was helping some of them.

"We were real close. We did almost everything together. Almost everything. Sometimes I wished I had played basketball just so I would have been there that day. Maybe I could have stopped it. Maybe it could have been me instead." It was like it wasn't me saying all this stuff. Like I was outside of myself watching myself talking about my brother. Did I really wish it would have been me that day? I wasn't sure.

"Rashid was the firstborn son and I was the baby. We liked it like that. He taught me a lot, but he still told me that I was smart and that he could learn from me, too. Everywhere, I was known as Rashid's little brother—more book smart than a student of the streets. Girls never did double takes to check out my five-five frame or bug eyes, unless I was with Rashid, who was blessed with the looks and personality of the ultimate player. But Rashid didn't mess around with chicks' emotions. He liked females too much to kick around their feels like soccer balls." When I said that, I heard some of the crew laugh a little. I started to feel a little more comfortable.

"That made the ladies love him more. Occasionally I would get some play off my brother's rep, but that was about as often as the Baltimore Ravens winning the Super Bowl." That made them really laugh.

"I know what you mean, bro," Oscar shouted. I looked up and saw, not a bunch of strangers, but people who seemed to really care. Natasha had a big smile on her face like she was proud of me. Dr. McKenzie was slowly nodding her head.

"Rashid wasn't a fighter either, but he commanded the respect of one. Cats knew he could scrap and that he stood up for what was right. He thought that violence was more than a last resort, it was a lazy one. That ain't to say Rashid hadn't blackened eyes and smacked up fools. Rashid was just smarter than the average dude. He understood the stakes and knew that his black skin and male status almost guaranteed him an all-expenses-paid stay in prison. Wasn't no cat on the streets worth his life. That was Rashid." I kept tapping my foot like it was keeping me on beat.

"My family was real close. We would eat dinner together. Go to church together. All types of stuff. We were like the perfect family." I took a long pause. I could hear the heat click on in the building. And I knew I was getting closer to the day that changed everything. My head returned to the ground.

"Um, not too long ago. It was Sunday. On a Sunday. He had gone to play basketball. Rashid loved basketball. He was good, too. I mean it was something he enjoyed doing, but he wasn't trying to be in the NBA or anything like that. On a Sunday, he went to the courts around our house. We lived in East Baltimore. That's where I grew up. Uh, something happened at the basketball court and when he was leaving, he was shot. He wasn't supposed to be shot, the bullet was meant for someone else, but it hit him instead." My legs began to feel weak. I wasn't sure if they were going to be strong enough to keep me standing. Dr. McKenzie must have noticed because she brought a chair over for me. I slid down into it and thought about that day. That Sunday. Usually when I thought about the day I was alone. In my bed. I started to feel unprepared.

"He died," was how I ended my story. Dr. McKenzie came over and thanked me for sharing my story and gave me a big hug. Natasha was up on her feet clapping. The rest of the crew joined her.

Then Dr. McKenzie allowed members to ask questions.

"Do you know who killed him?" Ramona asked with the tone of a reporter.

I was caught off guard by her question. No one had asked me that since my mother interrogated me that day. I stumbled for an answer. "Uh, no, I mean no. I mean if I did, things would be a lot different."

"How so?" Dr. McKenzie asked like she knew something she wasn't supposed to know. I was beginning to feel that familiar feeling of being trapped. I needed air.

For a moment, I zoned out. I didn't want it to happen. I didn't think it could happen. I thought I had used them all up. But I felt them forming at the corners. I clinched my eyes tight to try to stop the process. I was too late. Three tears—two from my left eye, one from my right—slowly glided down my face. The gates were opened. I was completely exposed.

"Yeah, would you seek revenge?" Ramona pushed.

"Naw, you would want to go the police," Oscar said.

"Police? Yeah, right," Walter added his two cents. "You would have to settle that in the streets. Five-o can't do nothing."

Voices started clashing at the same time. The four walls started to close in. Guilt hit me like a speeding bus. And something clicked inside me. I couldn't control it. Anger shot through my system and out my mouth.

"Shut up," I shouted. "All of you. You don't know what you're talking about." I started cursing everyone and everything. I shouted at the crew like they killed my brother.

Dr. McKenzie let me do it. She told the crew to let me get it all out. But I turned my anger toward her because she put me up to sharing before I was ready.

"Happy?" I said as I stormed out of the room. I heard people running after me, probably Natasha and Dr. McKenzie, but I was too quick. I heard them yelling for me to stop running. To come back. I kept moving like my life depended on it and ran out the back door.

When I pushed open the heavy wood doors separating the church from the world, the air hit me and charged my soul. My arms fell to my knees and my upper body followed. I was out of breath, but could now breathe.

I couldn't go back into the building and face my pain. So I got up slowly and started walking home, even more slowly. It must have taken me almost two hours.

When I arrived, my mother was a wreck. Her face was wet with tears. She had thrown a pair of jeans over her pajama pants.

"Oh my God," she exclaimed as she ran toward me. She hugged me like she used to.

"I'm fine," I told her.

"I was worried sick. Dr. McKenzie called me and told me what happened. I just got off the phone with the police. Your father is on his way home. He left work early because I told him you hadn't come home and that you ran out on your session. Do you know what you just put us through?" Her affection turned to anger.

It was my fault. Again.

She told me that I wasn't allowed to go to Straighten It Out anymore. I didn't object.

twenty-eight

breathe freely

I wanted to ask my uncle if I could stay. Maybe I could get a job at the art store. I thought about this while sitting on a bench in paradise. There was a slight wind that felt good when it hit my face. But these thoughts didn't last for long. The wind wasn't strong enough to blow away reality. An art store? Be for real. I looked at the tattoo on my forearm. My father had a matching one. Both read: *soldier*. It was the nickname passed down from my grand pops to my pops and now to me. When I was a boy, Peety called me "lil' soldier" until I grew into a big one. On my fifteenth birthday, it became official once the ink dried. But not really. I never grew into the name or the tattoo. An art store? Be for real, I said to myself.

As much as I tried, though, I couldn't forget why I was in Virginia. I couldn't forget what I did. One day I tried to write a letter to the kid I murdered. I knew slim worked at Moe's, but couldn't remember his name. So I asked my father. "Why you care?" my father said after I asked him. "I don't care," I lied. "I was just asking, you know, just in case the name comes up in the future, I thought it would be good to know." My father reluctantly told me.

The letter began:

Dear Rashid,
I don't really know what to write. Or what to say.
Maybe sorry? But if I was you, sorry wouldn't cut it.

I gave up on the letter after struggling with it for a few days. I decided to sketch a picture instead. I was only using a regular pencil, until my uncle drove me thirty minutes to an art store where I picked out charcoals. They made my hands dirty, but that made the art feel even more real. Sitting on my uncle's swinging benches on the front porch, I sketched an enormous horizon with a sunrise—one strong enough to capture everyone's pain and make anyone forget about the past. The horizon filled the page. There was no space for anything else. It was colorful even though it lacked color and heavenly even though it lacked religion. Heartfelt.

I started to feel again after spending nearly three months in Virginia. It wasn't long before my father told me it was time to come home and be a soldier. Return to East Baltimore feared. Respect for the gunman.

I looked around. My time was up. Art store? Be for real.

twenty-nine

Grave Digging

Rashid's grave was dirty. My mother grabbed the bottom of her lint-filled black coat and gently wiped the stone clean, like she was brushing strands of hair from her face. It looked like someone aimed a snowball of mud at the resting place. The *d* in Rashid's name and the *12* in his birth date were unreadable. This made my mother cry even more.

She asked aloud where the dirt came from. I wasn't sure if she was talking to me, so I didn't respond. I figured it was probably some kids playing around. Rashid was likable, so I knew it couldn't have been enemies wanting some type of sick revenge.

My father was waiting in the car, probably combing his beard with his fingers. That's what he did when he didn't have anything else to do. He came to the cemetery with us, but he only liked to visit Rashid's grave by himself. Usually at night.

I thought that was silly, but I was sure that Pops had his reasons. I never asked why.

Ever since my outburst at Straighten It Out, I had done a lot of thinking. I tried not to see Rashid as being in the ground lying six feet deep under dirt and a block with his name on it. I liked to picture him sitting on the bleachers at the basketball court where he got shot, watching whatever game was going on and shouting advice to the losing team. Or I would see him hollering at the cutie who worked at the chicken spot around the corner from our old house. She hooked him up with extra pieces and tons of fries. A lot of times, I would see Rashid laughing at my jokes like I was on stage and I had just said the funniest mess he had ever heard. I tried to see Rashid as living even though he was dead. It wasn't easy.

But my parents were another story. Moms insisted on visiting the place for dead people every Sunday— a ritual that I could do without. My father was spending more and more time alone. Like he didn't want to be around me or my mother. He didn't go to any more vigils and didn't ask about the progress of the case. I knew he cared, but he was doing a great job of convincing us that he didn't.

That day I rocked Rashid's black hoodie to protect

me from the cemetery wind that was always colder than the regular breeze. My nose was dripping, so I cleaned it with my sleeve. I stared at the busted Nikes I had on. They used to be the ones that Rashid balled in. They weren't the ones he had on that day, though. I planned on wearing them until my toes peeked through. I was never going to throw them away even if they looked like it was time for them to retire. Wearing Rashid's hand-me-downs was one of the ways I paid my respects. And it wasn't hard to do because Rashid's gear was always tight or at least he made everything he put on look cool. He could make a pair of off-brand jeans look hot. That was Rashid.

That's why I couldn't understand why my mother hung around in a creepy cemetery looking for him. It was cold and lifeless. Rashid was never any of those things.

I looked over at her. She was trying to light a candle in the middle of the day while the wind blew. Frustration took over her expression.

"This darn thing won't light," she said as tears exited her eyes and sped down her face.

I took toddler steps toward her. I wondered if I should help or allow her to continue to make a fool of herself. With each passing day, she and I got less and less close. And these days, she was liable to flick off—turn from a poodle to a pit bull in an instant. This could have been one of those moments. I was unsure. But I decided that helping her might make the time at the dead people's place pass a little quicker.

I shifted my back toward the lifeless wind. I turned the candle sideways and lit it with a red lighter that my mother probably copped at 7-Eleven. Once it caught the flame, I passed the candle to her and in the process, my phone started ringing. I had forgotten to put it on vibrate during the car ride over. My mother's face turned harder than Rashid's grave. Before I had a chance to turn off Kanye West's blaring voice, she slapped me across the face.

I had to fight my instincts to push her away from me. I glanced at the grave and thought about what Rashid would do. He would walk away. So I bounced and left my mother worshipping Rashid's grave like she was at a church altar.

Battling confusion, I slowly approached my parents' neglected '98 Nissan Maxima. The car still carried scars from the accidents it was involved in over the years. The ground was hard, although it was neatly trimmed grass. With each step I wondered whose son or daughter I was walking on top of.

I rubbed my face and wondered if there was any evidence left. The area where my mother popped me stung like crazy. But what hurt more was that she had put her hands on me like I wasn't her son. It wasn't one of those tough-love acts. She hit me like she didn't know me. Like I had something to do with my brother's murder. Then I thought about the secret I had buried. Would things be different if I spoke up? I was trying to protect us. My mother didn't know what Peety was capable of. I couldn't lose another person I loved. And neither could my parents. But that didn't excuse what she did.

My mother had never slapped me. Beating me and Rashid's asses back in the day when we got in trouble was different. Taking a belt to our backsides when we came home from playing outside after the streetlights came on was kind of justified. But this was mad disrespectful.

It had taken only one major beating—which took place in front of all our neighbors at one of our famous alley cookouts—for me to figure out that wigging out on my parents wasn't the move. I was eight. My mother told me to stop showing off—which was me talking too slick, disobeying what she said and acting like I had more rights than an eight-year-old kid should. The first smack delivered was a backhanded one from my moms. It shocked my system and I was embarrassed like hell. So much so that the only way I thought I could save face was by bragging to the dozen or so people still eating crabs, sitting on the back steps and chilling on picnic table benches, "That ain't hurt." My audience laughed, which only pushed me to go further when I should have stopped while I was ahead or behind. But I kept going. Rashid was ten and wiser than me. He tried to drag me into the house, but I thought I was on a roll and wanted to stay outside and give everyone a show.

My mother's response: "Oh, really? Well, since you want to act like a man tonight, you're going to get treated like one."

She went in the house and came back with my father. Raised old-school, my pops told me only once to "get myself together." I didn't. My father beat my behind, bare-assed, in front of everyone.

From that day on, I knew that my parents didn't play. They would double-team me if necessary. Rashid and I were good kids out of fear and respect.

My pops was sitting in the driver's seat with his head bowed. He was praying. He did that every day and more so since we lost Rashid. I didn't want to disturb him, so I leaned on the trunk. I pulled out my phone, flipped it open and texted Ricardo to remind him where I was. I thought about blaming him for getting me pimp-slapped, but I know it wasn't his fault. Ricardo's text response read, "My bad. I forgot. Hit me later."

A few minutes passed and my father rolled down his window to find out how long his wife would be. I shrugged my shoulders. I wanted to tell him that his wife had turned crazy, but I decided against that. The window went back up and my father bowed his head again.

After close to a half hour, my mother finally appeared. She acted like nothing happened. She was losing respect for the living—including those most important to her. She said more people should spend time at a cemetery. She said that she's pretty sure that if those underground had a chance to live again, they wouldn't concern themselves with crap that didn't matter. That's probably why she slopped together dinner at night instead of preparing the masterpieces she used to create. Or why she hadn't been to the hairdresser in months and had gained weight. She didn't care about the two giant holes in her stockings that came from her kneeling in front of Rashid's grave.

She got in the car without apologizing or even looking like she was sorry. We rode the fifteen-minute trip home in silence.

Once we got back to the house, I headed straight to my room without saying anything to the crazy woman. I slammed my bedroom door as hard as I could.

My room was a hot mess. Even if I decided to spend some time cleaning it, it would just become dirty again. So I didn't waste my time. In a swift motion, I pushed the clean clothes off my bed and leaped onto it back first, Nikes still on. I didn't care about the dirt from the cemetery that collected on the bottom on my soles. Anger increased my laziness.

I dialed Natasha's number and hoped to hear her comforting voice on the other end. I hadn't talked to her since Straighten It Out. I didn't really want to deal with what happened, but I had to talk to someone. I knew she could understand.

Her foster mother answered.

"Hi, Ms. Jameson, this is Avery. How are you doing?" If you called Ms. Jameson's house, you better understand respect.

"Hi, chile. I'm blessed," she responded in her usual Baptist manner. She would probably be a minister if she believed women were fit to lead churches. Instead she was a dedicated servant of First Covenant, a wannabe megachurch led by a flashy preacher who rolled around town in a Rolls-Royce.

"Is Natasha home?"

"We're just getting in from church. She is getting ready to help me with dinner, so she can only talk for a few minutes, but you and your parents are welcome to break bread with us."

Ms. Jameson is one of those sweet old ladies who constantly offered you food whether you wanted it or not. Sometimes I think she believed that food healed souls.

"That's nice, but I know my mother is cooking dinner right now." I lied. I knew asking to go over Tasha's would mean fighting with the crazy woman and I didn't have the energy for all that.

"Well, okay, then, but don't be a stranger," she said before handing Natasha the phone. I heard Natasha in the background tell Ms. Jameson that she'd pick it up in another room.

Ms. Jameson is also mad old-school. She doesn't own a cell phone, so Natasha definitely ain't got one. When Natasha first moved in with her hundredth foster mother, Ms. Jameson didn't have a phone put in her room. She had to use the one in the parlor room. I had no idea what a parlor room was, but it got a couch, a couple of chairs and a rug. So I guess it was just a fancy description for a living room. The entire house could be a museum. Ms. Jameson held on to a whole lot of ancient crap from way back in the day. Tons of black-and-white photos, old furniture and glass lamps cluttered the house.

But she kept it clean. No dust in sight. Well, actually, Natasha kept it clean. That was one of her responsibilities. Ms. Jameson told Natasha that she wasn't living in her house for free without contributing to the household. Every week Natasha had to sweep, mop and a whole lot of other stuff you couldn't pay me to do. But Tasha said she didn't mind because she got a lot in return, including a safe roof over her head.

"I have it, mam," Tasha said in her house voice, a mixture between proper talk and politeness. You had to speak the King's English in Ms. Jameson's house. At least that's what she always said.

"Hello."

"Hey, Tasha, it's Avery."

"Hey! I was so worried about you on Friday. Is everything okay?" She sounded like she was happy to hear from me. That was a good sign.

"Yeah, I'm fine. It was just a little too much for me, that's all." I didn't tell her that I might not be back to the sessions. "Were people talking bad about me after I ran out?"

"No, we were all real concerned. We knew how hard it was to talk about Rashid."

She said his name. And it sounded right.

"So what's up?" she asked me.

"Ain't nothin'. Just got back from the outdoor morgue." I grab Rashid's old basketball off my chipped nightstand. A few dirty cups fell onto the floor in the process. I didn't bother to pick them up. Instead, I focused on throwing the basketball in the air and catching it with one hand.

"Yeah? How are your parents doing today?" I could tell that Tasha was changing out of her church clothes by the movement on the other end of the line. For a split second I pictured her unbuttoning her blouse and showing a cute black bra underneath. Black had become my favorite color.

I ain't gonna lie. Tasha's body was banging. But she was also cool as a fan, not like those bourgie County girls at my school who expected you to pay for them to get their hair and nails done. But then turn their funky noses up at you if you worked at Mickey D's. Tasha ain't nothing like them. I had to remind myself that she and I were really good friends and that it was best to take things slow because of all that she had been through.

"My moms has officially lost her mind. She slapped me this morning because my phone rang while we were at Rashid's grave."

"For real? Damn, she's still taking his death pretty hard, huh?" There wasn't any more movement on Tasha's end and I figured she was lying on the bed, comfortable. For a moment, I dreamed that I was her sheets.

"Avery?" Tasha's voice knocked me out of this fantasy.

"Yeah, I am getting real close to getting into it with her. It's like she's not even my mother. She's become a different person. A person I really don't like."

"Don't say that. She's your mother. And she just lost her son. I mean I can't imagine how she feels. You all are a family and that's something to cherish. Some of us don't have a family. Together you guys can make it through this tough time."

Natasha said exactly what I needed to hear.

"So what you getting into today?" she asked.

"Nothing much. Ricardo wanted me to come over and hang, but I'm not sure if I'll be able to leave the house now. I always have to make up some lie anytime I go over there."

"I don't know why you are friends with him," she said.

"Why you say that?"

"I mean, from what you say about him, he doesn't seem like a very good person."

"He's definitely off the chain. But he's harmless." I defended Ricky and was a little upset that Natasha was judging him when she never met him.

"I'm just saying, who you hang around with says a lot about you."

"Well, Ricardo is the only dude who even came at me on the friend tip. I think that says a lot about him."

"If you say so." Pause. Longer pause.

"Damn, why you so hard on him and you don't even know him?"

"Look, Ms. Jameson is calling me," she said. "I gotta go." Just like that.

I was left confused. Women.

thirty

guess who's coming to dinner

MY mother didn't let me go to Straighten It Out the following Friday. I sat home, chilling in my room watching corny reality shows while she worked on her computer making a different flier with Rashid's picture on it. I was determined to get back into the program so that I could be around Natasha and not have to sit at home with my crazy mother.

Dr. McKenzie gave all the crew members her cell phone number, so I decided to give it a try and apologize for acting like an ass. I found her card in one of the pockets on my jeans and dialed.

"This is Robin," Dr. McKenzie answered the phone. She threw me off, so I asked to speak to her.

"Can I talk to Dr. McKenzie?"

"This is her." She sounded out of breath like she had been running.

"Uh, this is Avery."

"Avery, it's good to hear from you." She sounded for real. "I called your house a few times last week to check on you, but your mother said you were unable to talk." I threw my head back. Moms didn't tell me that Dr. McKenzie called after Friday. Now she was keeping stuff from me?

"I wanted to apologize for how I acted. I'm not sure what got into me."

"Do you want to talk about it?" That was one of Dr. McKenzie's favorite questions.

"No, I just felt bad and wanted you and the crew to know that I was sorry."

"We know you are, but I'm sure they would appreciate to hear it from you." The setup.

"Well, my moms kind of banned me from coming there because of what happened, but I was thinking maybe you could talk to her and change her mind."

"I am willing to talk to her because I do believe that you were making progress. I don't consider what happened a setback. But I do understand her concern. Do you want me to call her today?"

"Uh, no, um maybe you can come over for dinner

tomorrow?" I knew my mother wasn't going to be feeling the idea.

"Hmm, yes I would like that, as long as it's okay with your parents," Dr. McKenzie said.

"They're down," I lied.

My mother didn't care for the "shrink" coming over to try to "figure us out," but she agreed anyway. She prepared a boring meal of baked beans and hotdogs with toasted potato bread. That was fancy to her.

At first, we sat around the table without saying anything. Then Dr. McKenzie sparked some convo by thanking my parents and telling them how nice it was to have the opportunity to meet over a meal.

"We're glad to have you," my father replied. Then he asked her how she got into psychiatry.

"Well, I think psychiatry found me versus the other way around," she said before taking a sip of her iced tea. She was looking pretty nice in a skirt that wasn't all tight but still didn't look like an old lady would wear it. She had on her glasses, which made her look extra smart.

"I had a friend in high school who was depressed. At the time, I had no idea what depression was or how it's treated. I just thought he was always sad. But the sadness started to become worse and worse. He reached out to his parents for help, but they dismissed him. They didn't take his pleas seriously. I saw how much we as Black people don't take care of our minds the way we need to." Dr. McKenzie looked at my mother like she was talking directly to her.

"You're right about that," my father said.

"That's what partly pushed me to help people."

"That's nice," my mother responded like she didn't really care.

"Is that what made you start the youth support group?" my father asked. I wasn't sure if he was really curious or if he was trying to maintain some order around the table.

"Straighten It Out is my way to give back somewhat. A chance to compensate for the success of my practice in the County. I'll be the first to admit that health care isn't always affordable. And I've been blessed to run a business that does very well. Driving around in the fancy car and living in the fancy condo was nice, but it wasn't as fulfilling as I thought it'd be. I really had to reevaluate my life."

You could tell my mother didn't give a rat's ass. She was making a pile out of her beans. She was becoming bad at faking nice. I don't know if Doc noticed. She kept talking.

"While many of my friends from college spend their Friday nights at some overpriced theater event or having dinner overlooking Baltimore's harbor, you'll find me rocking jeans and a tank top listening to teenagers talk through their problems. And I love it." Her face lit up like car headlights. I don't meet too many adults who really like being around children. You can even tell that some teachers wished they had a different job by the way they look at you when you ask them a question in class.

"My friends have told me on several occasions that I need to get a life," she said.

"I admire your dedication," Pops told Doc. "We need people like you who genuinely care about our children." Doc smiled. Moms rolled her eyes and smashed some of her beans.

"Thank you. I'm just trying to do my part. Our kids need all of us to be there for them. And many of them just need a safe space to talk and be themselves. Straighten It Out may not look like much on the outside, but just like so many of my patients, on the inside, it's overflowing with potential."

My mother let out a long sigh like she was ready for dinner to be over. We all looked over at her.

"That's very impressive," my father said to try to cover up for my mother's attitude. "You're lucky to have found something you're passionate about," he continued. He had this weird look on his face and I wondered if he was flirting with Dr. McKenzie. But my father wasn't that bold or stupid.

My mother must have felt some kind of way, because she shot at Dr. McKenzie, "You don't think therapy is a bunch of crap?" Now if I had said something like that she would have reminded me of my home training. Who was going to remind her?

"Well, the word *therapy* throws many of us off—not just young people but adults as well. But we shouldn't let the word scare us into not seeking help when we need it. Therapy comes in many forms and many of them save lives. For example, Straighten It Out isn't standard 'therapy,' but it employs many of the field's principles and it focuses on those which are most engaging and effective for young people. At the most basic level, it's a safe space for young people to discuss their problems—many of which are pretty severe including the loss of loved ones, teen pregnancy, parents who abuse drugs and so on." My mother just grumbled. Doc ignored her. "When I first spoke to Avery, fifteen years of experience told me that pain was overwhelming him. I decided at that moment that I was going to help him whether he wanted it or not."

"You call my son running out of the room and going God knows where as helping him?"

"Human emotion can be unpredictable."

I decided to break in to get to the real reason why we were gathered.

"Dr. McKenzie has really been helping me with Rashid's death."

"Murder," my mother corrected me.

I ignored my mother. You could tell Dr. McKenzie was a little uncomfortable by the way she shifted in her chair.

"My wife and I really appreciate all that you've done for Avery," my father added to try to cut through the tension in the air. "It's been tough on all of us, but we've been trying our best to re-create our lives."

"Oh, I understand," Dr. McKenzie said with a smile.

"Understand? How could you possibly? Have you lost a child?" my mother asked.

"No, I haven't," Dr. McKenzie responded calmly. "But I understand the pain that's felt when one loses someone close," she said in a professional tone. She didn't lose her composure. I was surprised that she wasn't intimidated by my mother. I liked her even more.

"You doctors are funny," my mother said. "As if you can measure pain or compare one person's pain to another." My mother slammed a piece of hot dog into her mouth.

"I never said that. I do not practice pain comparison. It isn't fair and all it does is undervalue a person's feelings, which doesn't make my job easier. But I do know that most people experience an indescribable pain."

"She does know how it feels," I spoke up. And for

the first time in a long time, it seemed like I had my parents' attention. So I ran with it. "You act like you're the only one who hurts. You made me join that support group, but you're the ones who need the support. And then you tell me I can't go anymore when I'm just starting to get into it." I rose from the table with meaning and walked toward my room.

I heard Dr. McKenzie say that she would come and talk to me, but my father said he thought it was best that he came. I didn't hear my mother say anything. Doc had to walk herself out of the house.

My father came into my room with the same old speech about us being a family and things getting better. But I was tired of the empty words. I nodded my head like I agreed with him, but deep in my heart, I knew that nothing was further from the truth.

thirty-one

enough

It was Monday. Dante picked the wrong day to get buck. The last few weeks had wore me down. I had been walked over, disrespected, used, abused, singled out, misunderstood, judged, underestimated, provoked and challenged.

My fragile life was falling apart and I was waiting to take my anger out on someone. I was tired of running away or leaving the room. I was tired of feeling soft.

Ricardo and I were in the lunch line talking about nothing real important. Dante decided that he could just jump in front of me and I wouldn't say anything. I started out nice.

"Yo, man, how you just gonna cut like that?" I

asked in a joking way. Ricardo was right there to hype stuff up. "Yeah!" he said louder than he needed to.

"Whateva, man," he responded. Dante was on the hefty side but in a sloppy way. You could tell he ate more than he should and that he spent his time chilling in front of the television instead of running ball.

I didn't respond. I just took my rightful place in the line, in front of him.

Dante decided he was going to teach me a lesson. He shoved me. Not that hard, though, because I hardly moved.

But I took his action as supreme disrespect. He didn't have to take it there.

"What the fu—"Ricardo said after Dante pushed me.

I don't know what happened, but I charged after Dante like a bull. I grabbed him by the neck, pulled him to the ground and start whipping his ass.

I could hear Ricardo pumping me on. The rest of the students in the line were hollering like they were front and center at a Mayweather fight. The lunch ladies were yelling for help. But there was no stopping me. Aaron, one of Dante's boys felt the need to jump in and help his boy out. But Ricardo had my back like boys should. I didn't think he had any real fight in him, but he was doing his thing with Aaron, who was about a foot shorter than him.

Mr. Tinsdale, the vice principal, pulled me off of Dante. The gym teacher stopped the fight between Ricardo and Aaron.

Looking at us versus them, it was obvious that Ricky and I had smashed those fools. We were immediately sent to the principal's office. I didn't see where they took Dante and his boy.

For the first time in months, I felt brotherhood and I was reminded how good it felt.

In the principal's office, Ricardo and I were pumped. I felt like I had released mad anger that was pent up inside of me. I know it wasn't right to fight and it definitely wasn't something I normally enjoyed doing. But these weren't normal times.

"Yo, we were like a tag team back there," Ricky said as we gave each other pounds. He was mad hyper. I think it might have been his first real fight.

"I knew you weren't a punk from the first day I met you after Billy knocked you down. I saw a rawness in your eyes, you know?" I didn't really know, but I agreed anyway. "I'm tryna tell you, we're gonna make a killer team." He gave me another pound.

"We did our thing, didn't we?" I said with a slight smile.

"You and me, we're like brothers. Shoot, I always wanted a brother and never had one, and well..." Ricardo didn't finish. From the look on my face, he could tell that he was stepping over the line. I didn't want to go there.

"I'm just saying. It's me and you, we're our own crew, you know? Shoot, Boo ain't gonna be the only one with a crew. I'm building one. Right here and right now. Cats are gonna start recognizing."

"As they should," I said.

When I arrived home during the middle of the day, my mother was in her makeshift office, where the dining room was supposed to be. A tall beige file cabinet filled with paperwork stood in the corner. Each folder was neatly labeled and she developed a color-coded system to organize the documents in folders. Typed papers covered the glass table where we used to eat family dinners. Now on the rare occasions when we ate together, we squeezed at the cheap wooden table in the kitchen that's really for two people.

I didn't feel like hearing her mouth. I thought about catching the number fifteen bus to Silver Square Mall, but knew it was smarter to show up and face her and explain what happened before the school got a chance to call.

My entrance startled her. She was wearing brown reading glasses that were resting peacefully on the tip of her nose. Although she probably heard my keys, it didn't register that it could be her husband or son arriving home early. She immediately thought break-in. By the time she had an opportunity to react, I had the same mug on my face I had shot Dante before I stomped him.

"Boy, you scared the Jesus out of me," she said. She wasn't immediately concerned with what I was doing home so early. She pulled off her glasses and rubbed the stress from her eyes. Then she asked me why the hell I wasn't in school.

"I was suspended," I said like it was natural.

"What?" my mother asked. I knew that the question was really a way for her to give me an opportunity to explain myself before she went off on me.

I didn't follow the cue. She got up in my face. Her breath, which smelled like she hadn't brushed her teeth yet, assaulted me.

"I asked you a question. What happened?"

"I got suspended."

"Yes, we've established that. For what?"

"I got into an altercation." I used the word that Mr. Tinsdale had used. It didn't sound as bad as fight.

"Altercation?" She turned hysterical within a matter of moments. She probably visualized me in the same situation that got Rashid shot.

She looked like she was going to slap me again. But I grabbed her arm instead and she looked at me like I was crazy. Forget the fact that she had lost it a long time ago. I dropped her hand and stared her down. Then I turned around and went to my room. I wasn't going to take another hit from her.

thirty-two

Head Games

The next morning when my mother left the house to go to headquarters, I bounced. I wasn't about to be cooped up in my room every day of my suspension. I needed air and a reality check.

It was going to take three buses to get to Cut Me, me and Rashid's old barbershop. I used to hate riding the bus when I lived in the city. There was always someone who smelled like piss or it would be mad crowded so you were always up on somebody. But now, riding the MTA gave me a chance to be close to people who looked like they could live in my old neighborhood. Folks who carried stories in their eyes like they carried grocery bags.

I had started getting my hair cut in the County

when we moved out there, but it was never as tight as when Jerome at Cut Me hooked me up. The last time I got my hair cut, my line was all slanted like dude was drunk while he was shaping me up. Rashid was always serious about his cut and he got me to be serious about it, too. Every two weeks like clockwork, we were sitting in opposite chairs at Cut Me. Mike was Rashid's barber and Jerome was mine.

Being at Cut Me was more than just getting the fade tight, it was a chance to talk mess, learn from the old playas in the shop, argue over what side of town was hotter—East or West—and get put on to the latest mixtapes that were sold in the shop. Cut Me was like a school that taught real life. On any given day, you could learn about politics, women and stuff in between.

There were probably spots like Cut Me in the County, but I hadn't found them yet. Besides, I wasn't ready to find a new shop home. That was like looking for a new place to live and I was finding out the hard way that change wasn't all it was cracked up to be.

When I got to the spot, it was pretty crowded for a Tuesday afternoon. Probably because the shop is closed on Mondays. Black men of all ages were arguing over who was finer, Janet Jackson or Halle Berry. I took a seat in the front on the leather sofa. There were a couple of heads ahead of me waiting for Jerome.

Paul, one of the newer barbers, said, "Janet is classic." Me and the dude beside me both disagreed. Janet was fake to me. Halle had a natural beauty thing going on. Like Natasha.

"Plus Halle look like she don't get out of pocket either," Mike said.

"Man, don't get me started on attitude," John said. Everyone called him Crazy John. He worked around the shop, sweeping up hair and keeping the spot clean. I think he used to be on drugs but he was getting his life back in order. "That's what's wrong with Black women, too much damn mouth. Always want to tell you how to do something."

"Man, you just weak," Mike said. He was one of those cooler older dudes. He wasn't real old, probably like my father's age, but he acted like a young cat. "Black women are the strongest women there are. They hold you down. They raise little man if you gotta do a bid. They loyal."

"Loyal pain in my ass, that's what they are," Crazy John said. The shop exploded in laughter. He was always saying something off the chain.

Cut Me is on one of those typical hood blocks where a church is on one corner and a liquor store is across the street. But the shop is sick inside. It has huge mirrors and lights over them like the dressing rooms on television. The hardwood floors were shiny, and in the back there was a big-screen television and an even more comfortable leather sofa for when you had long waits. But I preferred to chill up front where all the action was.

No one messed with the shop because everyone knew it was owned by Mr. Henry, or Hen-Roc as he used to be known when he ran the streets like a kingpin. He was a fair old man, but folks knew not to get it twisted just because he went legit. He was still a crazy mofo who could handle business if necessary. He wasn't your average old-head. He rocked velour Sean John sweat suits, even in the summer— he said the material was cool in both senses of the word—Gucci sunglasses were always on top of his bald head, and a gold Jesus piece hung around a thin gold chain. I had met him the first time he took his chromed-out Cadillac to the car wash to "pretty up baby girl," as he would say.

Almost four months had passed since the last time Jerome cut my hair. When I sat in his chair, he investigated my head. "Got the busted shape-up, but that's okay. What can you expect in the County? Glad to see you haven't forgotten who really hooks you up."

"No doubt," I replied. "I haven't forgotten. It's harder to get over here, that's all."

"How your peoples?"

"They all right. Moms still taking it real hard, though."

While he was cleaning up the back of my head,

Jerome whispered to me, "You ain't heard this from me, but I heard that fool that ran up on your brother been seen chilling around town like he the man."

"He's back?" I asked with more than concern in my voice. I was loud enough for others to hear me.

"Young blood," Mr. Henry said, "let that be." I had no idea how he knew what we were talking about. But he knew things like that. He could probably smell my fear.

He was also known to dish out advice like a street psychiatrist—hood therapy was what everyone called it in the shop. As a former knucklehead who had been there and done that, Mr. Henry knew what he was talking about. He used his talents for good, quashing beef between rival dealers to try to maintain peace in the neighborhood that he always said he'd die for.

"You seen him?" I asked Jerome in a lower voice. I was trying to buy some time.

"Yeah, I seen him," he responded. "All comfortable walking around yo old neighborhood."

"Jerome, what I tell you about starting mess you can't finish?" Mr. Henry scolded his nephew.

"Oh, I could finish it, but it ain't my fight. Ya'mean? Rashid was cool, but he got a brother, feel me?" He waved his clippers in the air for emphasis.

"That's what's wrong with y'all young bloods," Mr. Henry began one of his speeches. "You right it ain't your fight, so why you bringing it here? If he go out and fight the fight as you suggest and end up in a box that would make you feel good?"

Jerome paused from cutting my hair. He hated when his uncle was right, especially about dealings on the street.

"Well, you sayin' he should do nothing?" he asked his uncle.

"I'm saying he should be smart. One moment of pent-up anger can change the rest of your life. Trust me. I've seen many a good men hauled off to prison like animals because emotion got the best of them. Use your head, young blood. Use your head."

That was good advice. But I wasn't sure what my head was telling me to do. The heavy feeling that came over me at the shop lasted the entire day. My worst nightmare seemed to be coming true. I knew eventually something had to give.

thirty-three

what's beef?

After the fight, Ricardo and I hung tough. I even had a little bop to my step around our school's hallways. We were both tired of people assuming they knew us or trying to take advantage of us because they thought we were weak. We started showing mofos the time. It felt good to feel like someone and it helped me put Trevor out of my mind. For only a little while.

"So did you decide about going to the party on Friday?" Ricardo asked me Monday morning when we returned from suspension.

"I mean, it sounds just like what I need." I was partly lying. I was still shook about Trevor being back. But I kept up the act. "You know? Get out a little. What time does it start?" I asked him. I was wondering if I would have to miss Straighten It Out. I was determined to go despite what my mother said.

"Eleven until," he responded.

"Eleven? You know my moms ain't going to let me out of the house at close to midnight."

"It ain't at night. It's during the day."

For a minute, I was confused. Then I got it. Ricardo had already started skipping school on a regular basis and kept trying to get me to join him. I hadn't yet, but wanted to. I thought quickly about my sad grades and my tripping parents. Hooking school wasn't a good look, but that's why I wanted to do it. I was tired of always doing the right thing. It wasn't getting me anywhere.

Ricardo continued hyping it up. "Yo, the party is gonna be like that. Chicks for days. Free liquor. Some of that maryjuwanna that you need to get up on. 'Cause let's be real. Your peoples ain't gonna allow you to do nuthin' anyway. You can finally meet my man Boo. There might even be some peoples from around your old way. It'll be like a hood reunion."

What did I have to lose? It was just a party. I gave my boy a pound.

"I'm in."

Tasha had asked me to stop by her house after school that day. I wasn't sure what she wanted, although I hoped it was something that would get us closer. But even if she only needed to rest her head on my shoulder, I was down.

I met her at her house. Ms. Jameson was at Bible study and Tasha was supposed to be at dance class. She opened the door and pulled me inside. I thought that was a good sign.

"Well, hello to you, too," I joked with her. She had on one of her dancing leotards with those big socks that came up her legs. You could see every curve and dent in her body. I got excited.

"Hey," she spat out.

"What's up?" I asked. "You sounded, I don't know. You sounded weird on the phone. Is everything okay?"

"I have something to tell you. And I've finally gotten the strength to do it, so please, please don't interrupt me."

I sat down on the antique-looking couch in Ms. Jameson's parlor room. I started to bite my nails while Tasha began to speak.

"My cousin came to pick me up on Friday after our session. Usually we go to get something to eat afterwards. He said he had to make a stop first. We went over to the Eastside. I wasn't sure what street we were on."

She was talking mad fast. It was hard for me to keep up.

"The houses all look alike over there. We stopped and this dude comes over to the car and my cousin says, 'What up, Trevor?' And they give each other a pound."

"What?" I jumped up. The room started to get small, real small. Tasha was the only person I had confided in about knowing who killed my brother. Regret started to hit me quick.

"Please let me finish first." She grabbed my hand and helped me back onto the couch.

"I wasn't sure if it was, you know, *that* Trevor. He said he was waiting on his father. Then Boo says, 'Tell Peety that I got to holla at him about some business.'"

I felt like a truck had just smashed into me.

"Wait, your cousin's name is Boo?"

"Yeah, why?"

I didn't respond. Everything was too messed up. I was caught in some twisted movie plot. Except this was my life.

"Trevor looked in the car and looked right at me. My entire body tensed up. My mouth locked shut. He asked Boo if I was his girl. He looked me up and down. It made me feel sick. Boo is really overprotective, so he shut Trev..." She had trouble saying his name. "He shut him down. He was like, 'Much respect, playboy, but this is my cousin. You know how it is with family.' Trevor said, 'My bad,' and then extended his hand out to shake mine. He asked me how I was doing."

"You shook his hand? You shook my brother's murderer's hand?" She tried to grab my shoulders so I wouldn't get up, but I was too strong for her. I needed space. She was too close to me.

"I didn't know what to do," she pleaded. It looked like she was about to cry, but I didn't care. For the first time, I didn't care about how Natasha felt.

She started to look different to me. She touched him and was touching me. I walked into her kitchen. I needed something to drink. My throat and stomach felt like they were on fire. She followed me.

"Then Boo asked him if he was going around Willie's on Friday for his party. And Trevor said he was. Then they gave each other pounds and we drove off. I asked my cousin who Trevor was, just to make sure. I mean, I knew it was him, but I, I didn't want to believe it. He told me not to worry about it and then switched subjects, asking me how school was going. On the way home, I felt sick. Like I had looked death in the eyes. I kept thinking about you and it was all so unreal. I mean Trevor didn't seem like, you know, a murderer. I wanted to tell you that night. Call you, but I didn't know how to tell you. I even threw up. And I know that Baltimore is small—my quote, unquote, reputation taught me that. But I would have never guessed that my cousin was friends with the boy who changed your life. I mean I know that Boo is no angel. I know he hustles. I've always known that. But I didn't think he was into the violent part of the game. He's been the only constant in my life since I can remember."

I remained quiet as I leaned up against the sink. I was getting pissed that she was defending Boo and trying to justify why he and Trevor were friends.

"Even though he's only a few months older than me, he's the closest thing to a father I've ever known. His mother was the one who used to tell me about my mother. And when she was killed in that accident, he and I got closer because we were both motherless. He raised himself. He has nobody like I used to have nobody. He's the only real family I have. He promised me that if I was still in the system when I turned eighteen that he would take care of me and help me go to college."

She let the information slow-cook. Minutes passed before either of us said anything. Her face was wet with tears. But I couldn't make her feel better. I was trying to do that to myself. I walked out of the kitchen and headed back to the couch. She followed me again.

"I've decided to take off Friday and go to that party with Ricardo," I told her. Partly to make her mad. I know she didn't like me hanging with Ricardo. She thought he was a bad influence. Plus she thought it was important for me to get back on track with school.

She gave me a look to let me know she thought I was talking crazy.

"Didn't you hear what I said? Trevor might be at that party. That's the party Boo was talking about!"

"Yeah, and?" I was in tough-boy mode. "It's about time I run into Trevor myself. Everyone else has." I wanted that to hurt her.

"Are you trying to ruin your life? Or get yourself killed? What if Trevor is there? Then what?"

"Then I'll handle it," I said like it was nothing.

"Handle it? Or you're a gangster now?"

"Whateva. What you think I'm a punk?"

"What are you talking about? Who do you think you are?" Truth was, I wasn't sure who I was.

"I know I ain't no punk. Not anymore. If Trevor's there, I'm gonna take care what I should have taken care of a long time ago." I didn't know how, but I would figure that out.

"Who's gonna protect you? I know you don't think punk ass Ricardo's gonna have your back."

"Oh, so now you're making me into some little naive cat who ain't got any street smarts?"

"What are you talking about? You're not even making sense." She was trying to turn things around on me.

"Whateva. I ain't saying I'm asking for beef. I'm

gonna get my little drink on, post up, maybe holla at a few chicks." That last part I didn't really mean. But the damage had already been done.

Natasha's face spelled disappointment.

"I meant from yourself. Who's going to protect you from yourself?" She fell back onto the couch with her arms folded across her chest.

"It ain't that deep," I declared even though I knew that was a lie. "The last few months have been pure hell. I deserve to get my party on."

"You mean you're going to cut school, get drunk and high and possibly get into some beef or kill just because you've had a hard week?" Natasha didn't look at me as she roared her thoughts.

"Damn, you want me to be one of those good guys who watches life pass him like it's a bus or something?"

"Where is all this coming from?" Natasha snapped. "It's like I don't even know who you are right now." She looked at me like she didn't recognize me. I was supposed to be the guy who gave her hope that not every male put their rep before common sense.

"No one is telling you not to live your life, but will you listen to yourself? You sound crazy."

"What, are you jealous? Like now that you're a good girl and all, you can't get loose anymore?" She looked like she wanted to smack me like my mother did. I instantly wished I could take my words back. "My bad. I didn't mean that. My brother told me to start living my life. And I intend to. This party isn't a big deal, but it's a start. Ricardo says—"

"I still can't believe that you're listening to Ricardo. He's a fool who thinks life's a game. He's a bored rich kid who doesn't understand what life is really about. Life ain't about frontin' like you're hard, trying to be down with some crew or wasting it away getting high."

"Why are you getting on Ricky like that? This ain't about him. I've learned over the past few months that we don't get any do-overs. This is it. Right here!" I clapped my hands for emphasis.

"And that's why you have to be smart in this life."

I was tired of the lecture. I was tired of people telling me what to do and how to live my life. I of all people knew how fragile life was. "I'm outta here," I said without giving her a hug or looking in her eyes. I just bounced.

thirty-four

I USED TO LOVE HER

Natasha and I didn't speak all week. What was there to say? Lots. But I didn't want to be the one to say any of it first. Plus I had mad stuff on my mind, including the fact that I had agreed to go to a party where I knew I could possibly run into Trevor. That scared the shit out of me. I still hadn't decided what I would do.

"I told my friend Natasha about Boo's party," I told Ricky. We were chilling at his house, watching videos, talking about Friday and drinking beers.

"What you do that for?" he asked with a little bit of alarm in his voice.

"Yo, she's cool," I said, although I was unsure

how true that was anymore. "Actually, she already knew about it. Boo's her cousin. Isn't that a trip?"

Ricardo's head popped back. "Natasha? Wait, she got a phat ass?"

"Yeah, I guess," I said as I took a swig from my brew.

"Oh, shit. That's the Tasha you've been talking about the whole time? The 'queen' you wanted to rescue? Sorry, homey, but I ran through that already. I hit it like a car in an accident."

"What?" I didn't believe what I was hearing.

"When was this?"

"A few months ago. I met her at the movies one day. Got the digits, invited her over and then knocked it down. Man, she's got some sweet stuff. You should definitely hit it. Cause you know the saying, 'Ain't no fun if the homies can't have none.'" He held his hand up to give me a high five.

I threw my beer bottle at Ricardo's wall. I had been mad a few times in my life. But words couldn't describe the anger that burned inside my body.

"Whoa, what the hell?" he screamed before he started laughing. "Now that's the Avery I know. The one with fire in his blood."

"Yo, you're lying?" My voice sounded like a roar of a lion.

"If I'm lying, I'm flying," Ricardo replied. "Man, she's just a freak. But you and I, we're brothers." He whipped out his phone and showed me a picture of her that he had on his phone. She was smiling big in the camera like she smiled at me.

"Man, you've been hoodwinked! Bamboozled. She's had like half of Baltimore. Forget her. Can't turn a ho into a housewife." Ricardo thought the entire situation was hilarious. "Remember what I told you, bros over hos." He patted my back. And I started to think he was right. I tried to hide how hurt I was. I didn't want Ricardo thinking I had fallen for a chicken.

I had almost forgotten why I started telling the story to Ricardo in the first place. I took a deep breath and tried to block the last five minutes out of my mind. "Anyway, she said that word on the street is that Trevor is going to be at the party. Did you know that he and Boo were cool?"

Ricardo gave me a funny look. I couldn't read it. Then he said, "Naw, I didn't know they were cool, but shit. This is our chance to smash that fool. I wouldn't be surprised if Trevor didn't hook up with Tasha either. That's how she gets down. With everybody. Man, too bad you didn't get a chance to hit that. But don't worry about it. There will be plenty of ass tomorrow."

The mention of Tasha and Trevor in the same sentence made me feel like someone just punched me in the stomach, then kicked me while I was on the ground.

Ricardo went into his closet and pulled down one of his limited-edition Nike shoe boxes. He opened it and pulled back the white tissue paper. There was a gun. A big, black one. I wasn't skilled on pieces, so I didn't know what type it was. I actually had never seen one up close like that before. I knew my father had one for protection, but he never showed it to me and Rashid.

"If anyone gives us trouble, I got it." I actually smiled like the thought of what Ricky was suggesting made me happy. I nodded my head in agreement. I was tired of hearing about Trevor parading around the city like my brother's life meant nothing. The cops had more than enough time to arrest him and they did nothing.

"It's time for me to grow into my name, Ricky Ross. You know what I'm saying?" He rubbed the gun like it was a female.

I actually did know. I looked down at the gun. It was time for me to grow in life. My mind was racing like the cars do up Northern Parkway. Natasha lied to me like I was some sort of chump. As much as I talked about Ricardo, she never mentioned knowing him and of course she never mentioned that they had hooked up. All I could think about was what they might have done together. It made my stomach do somersaults. Telling me she and I couldn't become closer because we were building something. All the while she was knocking down my homeboy.

It was the second worst day of my life.

Tomorrow, it was gonna be on at the party. That, I knew for sure.

thirty-five

party for the right to fight

That morning I awoke to my parents' arguing. The shouts were louder and more intense than usual. I tried to zone out and listen for a sign from Rashid. He hadn't spoken to me since that night. But I kept listening. It was hard to think or concentrate in the chaos. I needed to take drastic measures. I decided that I would just start over. It was going to be the first day of my life.

Ricky texted me at 6:45 a.m. to tell me how hyped he was and that he would meet me at 8:00 right after my mother dropped me off. The plan was to hop in his car right after she left.

I got up like normal and got dressed. That morning

I really put thought into my outfit. It took me a nice minute to pick which one of Rashid's shirts I was gonna rock.

I decided on a sweet blue-and-white button-down, my big boy Rocawear jeans and the fresh kicks I had copped when Ricardo and I went shopping. I had begun spending Rashid and my savings stash. I figured that I might as well enjoy it.

My mother was already at her "office" when I finished dressing. No breakfast was made. I grabbed a banana. While she drove me to school, we didn't speak until she told me that she had decided to allow me to go to Straighten It Out that night.

"Cool," was all I said. I would think of a way to get out of that later. Right now I was focused on getting to the party without getting caught.

She dropped me off like it was a regular day. I waited for her to drive off and go back to the house where she continued to do nothing. I walked around the side of the school and saw Ricardo waiting in one of his peoples' cars, the 5 Series BMW. The ride was sweet. Ricky didn't have his license yet, but he claimed he had been driving since he was eleven. I hopped in the car like I owned it.

Once we got off our school's street, Ricky blasted the radio. The rapper Rick Ross rhymed about hustlin'. It was Ricardo's favorite song. I jammed to it and let the beat take over.

The party was at this row house about five blocks from my old street. It felt good to be back around the way. But it wasn't long before all of the baggage that the Eastside carried hit me. Being around the way meant I was back where it all started. It meant that Trevor could be feet away. I needed something to relax me.

"You all right, playboy?" Ricardo asked as he parked his father's car a few doors down from the house.

"Yeah, I'm good." It didn't look like much was going on at the house, but I guess that was the point.

Ricardo knocked on the door like he was doing a hip-hop beat. A thick-necked dude wearing a faded black tee opened the door with a suspicious look on his face.

"Ten bones a piece," he barked.

"What up, Bam? It's me Ricardo. We met two weeks ago at Tyrone's." Ricardo flashed a pretty-boy smile, but Bam didn't return it.

"Yeah? Still ten bones a piece." Big neck wasn't messing around.

Ricky laughed a little. I wasn't sure if he was gonna start somethin'.

"Okay, playboy," he said. He pulled out a twenty and paid for us.

Big neck stepped outside and the joint was already jumping. Liquor—dark and light—lined the kitchen table. A bag filled with weed was chilling by the red plastic cups. Lil Wayne banged at just the right volume so that the party was crunk, but not enough to alert nosy neighbors or 5-0. There was like thirty or so people already getting their chill on.

Ricardo was pumped. He gave a few dudes a pound as we headed to the kitchen to fix our drinks. I had only started drinking Coronas at Ricky's house. I still hadn't had any hard liquor, the real stuff. But that was all that was on the table. Vodka. Henny. Patrón. I wasn't sure which one to take.

"I'll make the drinks," Ricardo said. I was glad I didn't have to make a decision.

I looked around the room. There were definitely two times more dudes than females. But the chicks who were there gave off that down-for-whatever vibe. I caught the eye of one of them and she flashed me a sexy smile. The old Avery would have turned away. The new Avery motioned for her to come over.

She strutted like a model over to the kitchen. Ricky handed me a drink. I took a sip and it tasted like medicine mixed with orange juice. But I drank it anyway. He asked me who my new friend was. I didn't know her name, but she whispered, "Dionne," in my ear. Her tongue touched my skin and sent a warm feeling through my stiff body. I was starting to feel real good.

I chatted with Dionne like an old-school pimp. I told her how good she looked in her Baby Phat jeans.

"Stop nursing it," Ricardo said as he pointed to my cup. "There's more from where that came from." I downed the drink. My throat felt like I had swallowed a bowl of hot soup.

"Now it's time for shots." He poured the three of us some Patrón. We clicked our red cups like they did on television. Then downed the shots. Dionne went from cute to fine in a matter of minutes. Everything looked bigger and better.

Ricardo suggested we go check out the rest of the spot. As we walked out the kitchen—Dionne in the front so we could check out what she was working with—he handed me a strip of rubbers.

"Let's see what type of new man you really are." I snatched the condoms out of his hands and stashed them in my pocket.

As we walked into the living room, dudes were laying back enjoying life. Smoking. Drinking. Watching movies on the flat-screen television. Most of them looked like they were hooking school just like Ricardo and I. Others looked like they were finished with school, while others looked like they stopped stepping inside a school a while ago.

"There's Boo," Ricardo said. I looked over to finally get a view of the kid who I knew so much about but never met. And there was Natasha. Standing right next to him.

Part of me was excited to see her and wanted to

forget about all the crap between us. She was looking right. She had on one of those girlie hoodies that was tight in the right places. Her jeans stuck to her like paint. Hair pulled back in a clean ponytail.

"There's your girl," Ricky said as he elbowed me in the stomach. And then I realized I couldn't forget.

I told Dionne I would get with her a little later for some alone time. Ricardo and I went over to the cousins. Natasha met me halfway.

"What's up, girl? Long time no see," Ricardo said.

She had a puzzled look on her face. "Can I talk to you alone?" she asked me.

Ricardo shook his head and snickered. He went over to chat with Boo.

"Is there someplace quieter where we can talk?" she asked me again since I ignored her the first time. I shrugged my shoulders. She grabbed my hand and walked me upstairs.

Boo mean-mugged me as I walked upstairs with his cousin. I just rolled my eyes. Let him think what he wanted.

It was still early, so we managed to find an empty bedroom. Natasha closed the door. My head had started to spin. Seeing her messed it up even more. I sat on the twin bed. It was neatly made and covered with a purple blanket.

"Why are you here?" I asked her.

"I care about you, Avery, and I didn't want you

to make any mistakes. I had a dream last night that something really bad happened to you. You shouldn't be here."

I cut her off like a bad driver.

"You don't, huh? Well, you know what I don't think is a good idea? Letting cats run through you like a car wash."

She looked surprised. Then the veins popped out of her forehead. Her bright eyes turned gray.

"What?" She looked away from me.

"Now it all makes sense. How you used to talk so much shit about Ricardo. That's because you let him hit."

"Excuse me?" She pressed her hand to her hip.

"Oh, don't act stupid," I said with a rage I couldn't identify.

"What are you talking about?" she asked. "You're drunk."

"And you're still lying. Care about me? You don't give a damn about me. You played me like some sucka." My anger was so explosive it was hard to direct it.

She sat down on the bed next to me and put her hand on my thigh. I brushed it off and got up to head for the door.

"I met him at the movies during the summer. Boo had dropped me and Ramona off and Ricardo was with him. Ricardo told Boo he was going to go ahead and catch a movie, too. He ended up paying for Ramona and me and chilling with us. He was funny and nice. We exchanged numbers and he called me every day. We talked about all kinds of stuff. I liked him."

I didn't want to hear any more. I started walking again.

"I never said I was perfect. That doesn't exist. I know I should have told you, but I didn't want us to stop being friends. I was ashamed, too. He was chillin' with me to find out more about my cousin, Boo. When I didn't have sex with him, he stopped calling. I was so close to telling Boo, but I know my cousin. And Ricardo ain't worth it."

"You think I'm gonna believe you now? Ricardo told me y'all hooked up."

"We didn't," she sang out. "I swear on my mother's life."

I knew she was telling the truth when she said that. But my head was all messed up. Why would Ricky lie like that?

My world was spinning and so was the room.

"I need some air." I left Natasha crying on the couch. As I walked down the steps, Boo was coming up.

"Where's my cousin?" he asked in a tone that told me he wasn't on joke time.

"In there." I motioned to the bedroom. He moved

past me and I walked down the steps. The party hadn't stopped. It looked like everyone else was either drunk or high or a combination of the two.

Ricky was chilling on the couch with some breezy. Dionne was in the middle of the living room floor moving like an intoxicated video girl. Patrón was guiding her hips. Dudes were clocking her heavy. Her body was like whoa and it was moving like it was calling me. I decided that after I got a little water, I would get up on that. I was sure she could make me feel better. I walked into the kitchen and got some water from the sink. Between the alcohol and the drama, I felt like I was going to throw up.

Then I heard it. The name that made me drop my cup on the floor.

"What up, Trevor?" I heard someone say in the living room. It took me a little while to turn around. I knew that doing so meant I was going to be meeting my fate. I did slowly. There he stood. Only fifteen feet away from me. He had on a black fitted cap, black T-shirt and black jeans. Like he was mourning. Diamond earrings shined in his ears. I thought about ripping them out. He was talking to two dudes who looked like they were laughing at everything he was saying. I looked over at Ricardo who was still in that girl's face. I didn't know whether to attack or fall back and calculate my approach.

I downed some more water and ran the sink to

splash a little on my face. I was about to turn around again, but I felt a punch in the back of my neck instead. The hit took the wind out of me.

"You think you can play my cousin and get away with it?" Boo was on top of me, beating me like he was my father.

I saw Ricardo out the corner of my eye. He was standing there. Doing nothing. Everybody else watched. No one was going to stop Boo at his own party.

Natasha came running over and grabbed her cousin's back. "Stop!" she kept yelling. "He didn't do anything!"

Boo stopped throwing blows and left me on the floor. "You were crying, Tasha," he said out of breath. "What was I supposed to think?"

"You were supposed to find out why I was crying, not go and beat someone up like some animal."

I felt her lift my head into her lap. I wasn't sure if I was bleeding. But my body hurt like it.

Boo reclaimed his senses and came over to help me up and get me to the couch. The party went back to business. Like nothing happened.

Natasha made a bag of ice to put over my face. She started patting my eye. I pushed her hand away.

"I'm fine," I told her even though I was on fire.

I looked around for Trevor but didn't see him. Instead I locked eyes with Ricardo, my "brother." I got up. I could hear Natasha asking me where I was going, but I didn't answer her. I asked Ricky Ross if I could holla at him for a minute in one of the bedrooms upstairs.

As soon as we got alone, he was back to talking trash. "Yo, that was crazy about Boo. I was just about to jump in when Natasha came."

I nodded. I wasn't there to hold a conversation. If I had time, I would have dug into him. But I was focused on one thing.

"Yo, where's the gun?" I asked him calmly.

"Right here." He lifted his yellow T-shirt and showed me the weapon.

Before he had a chance to drop his shirt, I grabbed it.

"Yo, what you do that for?" He threw his hands up like I was going to aim it at him.

"I'm gonna hold on to this," I said as I put it under my shirt. "It's not like you're gonna use it, bro." I looked him in the eye in a way that made him drop his head and stare at the floor.

"My bad, I—"

I put my hand up to silence him. Then I walked out of the room with the gun. I already felt different. My body still ached from my beat down, but I was packing now. What?

I went looking for Trevor. Downstairs was crowded like a club. Twice the amount of people occupied the spot. Dionne appeared in front of me, rubbing my chest. She asked me if I was okay and if there was anything she could do to make me feel better. For a moment, I thought about abandoning my plan and finding a room to see if Dionne could back up her talk. I resisted.

"I'm good. Look, I have to do something right quick, but let's hook up in like a half." Dionne smiled and switched her hips toward the basement.

I continued searching the room. I didn't see Trevor. I saw Natasha. She ran up to me, talking a mile a minute. I told her to chill out and that we would smooth things over later. But as far as I was concerned I was done with all of them. Natasha. Ricardo. They both were out of my life after today. At that moment, though, I needed her.

"I need you to do me a favor," I asked her. "I need you to find Trevor and get him to go in a room with you."

"What?" Her eyes widened.

"No, not like that," I tried to reassure her.

"I'm not gonna be a part of you getting in some beef," she said.

"Look. I'm in no shape to fight, remember?" She flashed a guilty face. "I just want to talk to him. I deserve that much."

She was trying to read me. And I was putting on a real performance. I softened my face and grabbed her hand.

"Okay," she said hesitantly.

I told her to check the basement for him and to bring him into the back bedroom. That gave me enough time to clear it out.

We parted ways. I felt like I was in charge of my life. I was dictating how things were going to turn out.

I headed to the bedroom. There were two girls in it changing out of their school uniforms. I waited for them to finish and then locked the door behind me. It took nearly twenty minutes, but finally Tasha knocked on the door three times like I told her to. I stood on the side of the door so that when they opened it, they wouldn't see me.

I heard them laughing and Trevor saying something about how much he had been wanting to get at her since he met her in Boo's car that day. I held the gun tightly. It was my first time handling one. It was heavier than I expected. Cold.

Who was the punk now? I wondered but wasn't gonna ask. I remained silent.

Trevor walked in first. Natasha stopped at the doorway. I closed the door in her face. Then locked it.

Trevor turned around to a gun in his face. Our eyes met. Seconds passed between us like colds. I could hear the fear in his heart. I could hear him breathing.

He lifted his hands in the air and started pleading for his life.

"Shut up," I said forcefully. He did what I said.

"Sit down." He did what I said.

"Do you know who I am?" He shook his head although he looked like he recognized my face.

"So you go around killing people and you have no idea anything about them?"

Trevor clinched his eyes and dropped his head. For a quick moment, my life scanned before my eyes. Rashid and I as kids eating snowballs. Rashid and I on Christmas opening our gifts while our parents watched with huge smiles on their faces. The four of us eating dinner together. Laughing together.

First the tears, then the anger.

I thought about pulling the trigger.

Trevor raised his head and his face was wet. The look he gave me threw me off. His eyes were puffy and weak, not hardened like I expected. I kept the gun pointed in his direction, but it was becoming heavy. Too heavy. I needed answers.

"Why?" I yelled. It was the question that had been burning through my mind since the day Rashid died.

After wiping tears from his eyes, he began to speak.

"I wish I knew why," he said while wiping his eyes. "I ask myself every day. Why?" He covered his face with his hands and took a deep breath. "I know it probably doesn't mean much, but I wish things happened differently that day. I didn't mean to..." He paused for what seemed like years even though it was only a few seconds. "I didn't mean to shoot Rashid. I wished I had never went back to my car. I didn't want to shoot anybody. I don't know what happened." Then he looked up at me and said, "If I could go back in time and change things, I would."

I lowered the gun a little and leaned on the dresser in the room. I felt drained.

"He was my brother," I cried out. "He didn't deserve to die."

"I know, I know, I know, I know, I know," was all Trevor kept repeating. He held his stomach with one hand and his forehead with another. I was starting to believe him.

Then the door was kicked in. Police officers stormed the room. I immediately dropped the gun and held up my hands. Two cops tackled me to the ground and another got Trevor. The house was being raided.

Detective Sanders remembered me from that day he lectured my mother and I. He had received a "tip" that Trevor was going to be at the party, so he arranged the raid to bring him in for questioning. Apparently he was onto Trevor as a possible suspect. We were in a small gray-colored room at central booking, a place I thought I'd never end up. He was sweaty like usual and he needed to shave, badly.

"What were you doing in the room alone with Trevor and a gun?" he asked me.

I knew I should have waited for a lawyer, but I was too tired. I just wanted the entire day to be over with.

So I told the truth. "Talking." He looked at me with a crooked eye.

"Whose gun was it?"

"My friend…uh, this kid Ricardo's."

"What did you and Trevor talk about?"

Finally, it was my moment to say what needed to be said. I didn't hold on to my pain any longer. "He confessed to killing Rashid." Once I said it, I wondered why it was so hard for me to do. The words didn't get all choked up in my throat, they came out smoothly.

"Would you testify?" he asked.

"Yes," I said without hesitation. It was as simple as that. For the first time in months, I felt relieved. Guilt no longer followed me.

There was a knock at the door. An officer led my father into the room.

"Son," he said as he gave me an air-sucking hug. "I was so worried about you. Your mother left this frantic message and the only words that I understood were Avery, jail and gun. I jetted out of the post office and I just kept having these flashbacks of driving to the hospital to see your brother. Is your mother here?"

"Not yet," I said. My father finally let go of me.

"I'll leave you two alone," Detective Sanders said as he got up and walked past us.

My father didn't ask me any questions about how I landed in central booking. He was just happy that I was alive, in one piece.

My mother arrived a few minutes later. She rushed into the room like a storm. "Oh, thank God." She hugged my father and I simultaneously. Then she did something I hadn't heard her do in months. She started praying.

I lay in bed that night trying to understand the day's events. The police decided not to press charges. My parents and I had a long talk. A talk we should have had a long time ago. I apologized for messing up so badly. My mother apologized for neglecting me and obsessing over the wrong things. My father apologized for not being there for me like he thought he should. I didn't realize that for the most part, we all felt the same way: like we were going to explode. My father admitted that he thought about leaving, taking off to a place where no one depended on him, where he didn't have to put forth so much energy to try to make things feel normal. But then he'd see me and mother's face and he knew that his feelings were just the result of losing faith. I guess that was what I was trying to do by starting over.

That Friday marked another Straighten It Out session that I had missed. And it was on a day when I needed to be there so that Dr. McKenzie and the crew could have talked some sense in me.

I had been looking at things all wrong. I thought Ricardo was someone whom I could consider family, but how could I when he didn't even know the meaning of family?

I thought about how badly I treated Natasha—she was my real family. I missed her so much I could feel it in my bones. After the day's events, I realized how important it was to live and think in the moment. So I picked up the phone and called her.

outro

TIME IN

WE weren't moved back into our old house long before my mother called me into the kitchen. She was fixing bacon and eggs for us to eat before my father and I headed to the courts to shoot around.

"A letter came for you," she said, her hair still in rollers. Her eyes told me who it was from. I took the white envelope from her hand without looking at it.

"Let me know if you want me to read it with you."

"Thanks," I said while my hands started to sweat. I wiped them on my hoodie.

My father strolled in wearing sweats and a Morgan State T-shirt.

"Ready, son?" He grabbed my mother by the waist, turned her around and kissed her on the lips.

In counseling, Dr. McKenzie told us that we should start doing the things we used to do again. So my parents, they were always getting their kiss on.

"Uh, in a minute, I just have to uh, do something real quick."

My mother and I looked at each other and she shook her head to tell me it was okay to go read the letter.

The walk to my room felt crazy long. Images of Rashid flashed in my head. It was like I could see him in the hall walking beside me, encouraging me to do what had to be done.

When I finally reached my room, I sat on my bed. Envelope next to me. Facedown. I thought about calling Natasha for support while I read the letter, but thought it was probably something I should do on my own.

Even though I had got it all wrong, trying to be someone I wasn't, I still tried to keep some of the confidence that I gained as an improved Avery Washington. That's what I told myself. I could do it. I could open the envelope. I could read the letter.

I banged my chest and remembered who I was. I turned the envelope over. His name stared back at me. Trevor Butler. I smoothed my face with my hands and took a deep breath. Slowly, to make sure I didn't rip the letter inside, I carefully opened the envelope. Then I pulled out the piece of paper. I let it sit on the bed a little while I looked at the window. There were three kids walking down the alley laughing. Reminded me of my brother and I talking trash with one of our friends. I smiled. It felt good to be back home. But that didn't mean that everything was perfect. Far from it. The letter on the bed was evidence of that fact. I let five minutes pass. My father hadn't asked again if I was ready. I was sure my mother told him what I was trying to do.

Another deep breath. Then another. I patted the letter with my fist. Then picked it up. I unfolded a third of it. Then the second third. Before I knew, I was staring at Trevor's handwriting.

Dear Avery—

People around the way don't understand my decision. But for some reason, I think you probably do. Turning myself in was the only way I was going to get a new life. I was tired of frontin'. I wanted a new life. Not necessarily in prison, but maybe now I'll be able to free myself from myself. If that's true, then I pray it will be worth the sacrifice.

You're probably wondering why I'm writing you. Truth is, you saved my life. You could have blasted me. Did to me what I did to your brother. But you didn't. You gave me a second chance. If I could go back in time, things would be different. I wouldn't be here and you wouldn't be reading this letter.

I wanted to put into words how I felt about everything that has happened and how bad I feel about forever changing your life.

But I'm not much of a writer, so I drew something instead. I hope it says what I cannot.

Trevor

Turn this over.

I flipped the letter. It was a picture of a sunrise.

QUESTIONS FOR DISCUSSION

1. Throughout this story, Avery desperately tries to hold on to memories of his brother, Rashid. What would you suggest that Avery do to maintain his memories of his brother?

2. Why do you think Ms. Rosalie does not tell Yvette, Avery's mother, who killed Rashid? Do you consider Ms. Rosalie a friend? Yvette vows to never see her friend Ms. Rosalie again. Is Ms. Rosalie's friendship worth keeping?

3. After his brother's funeral and his family's move to Baltimore County, Avery says that his family was "moving on without moving on." What did he mean by that statement? Was this a good decision for Avery's family? Why or why not?

4. In Chapter 26, Avery and Natasha realize that they have a lot in common. What are some of the connections that help to draw them closer?

5. In Chapter 15, we get a glimpse of the kind of life that Trevor wanted—his dream of becoming an artist—and we know of Rashid's dream to go to college. How did Trevor's and Rashid's environments affect their realizing their dreams? What can

be done to help ensure that all young people realize their dreams?

6. Is Dr. McKenzie on the right track in helping young people? How does Dr. McKenzie help to change the lives of the young people in her group? Do you think that therapy can be beneficial to helping people overcome challenges in their lives? Why or why not?

7. When Avery meets with Trevor in the back room, what are Trevor's feelings when he talks to Avery? Both boys have many emotions that have built up since Rashid was shot. Do you think that, prior to seeing Trevor at the party, Avery should have sought revenge or told the police what he knew? Should Avery have attended the party? When the two boys meet, what feelings do they release? Why?

8. Throughout the story, Avery's parents' emotions change. How and why do you think his mother's emotional state deteriorates as the story progresses? How would you describe her character? What about Avery's father? How would you describe him?

9. Ricardo is also crying out for help. What characteristics does he exhibit that signal he's headed for trouble? Is his friendship with Avery a positive one for either of them? Why or why not?

10. Although she also exhibits some emotional problems, how does Natasha survive all that she has endured? What characteristics does she exhibit that give you the impression she is getting her life back on track? What can you take away from this story that can help young people overcome challenges?

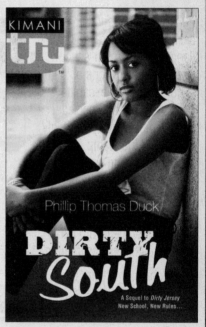

KIMA

LOVE.
FAMILY.
SCHOOL.
LIFE.
DRAMA.

IT'S ALL HERE.

www.myspace.com/kimani_tru

DATE DUE